UNFORTUNATE WOMEN

Beverly Van Horn

Cover Design: SelfPubBookCovers.com/SFCovers

The patients names and stories are fiction.

ISBN: 0967188563
ISBN: 9780967188560

Printed by Create Space, an Amazon.com Company
First printing 2017

DEDICATION

This book is dedicated to all the women
Who gave birth to a child
And gave it up for adoption.
She is considered a hero and
She has blessed many families.

ACKNOWLEDGMENTS

My editor, Jennifer Top, who had so much patience going through my manuscript and finding quite a few mistakes in just my thinking. For instance, she reminded me that World War 1 wasn't called that until we had the second world war.

I must thank my daughter-in-law Pam McPheeters for getting me even more encouraged when I read the research paper she wrote for the University of Missouri in Kansas City. I had been collecting materials but had not put them to paper.

I thank my daughter-in-law Priscilla McPheeters who let me publish the letter she wrote about her mother who was born at The Willows.

I thank my daughter, Leilani Holmberg for her editorial comments.

I thank my cousin, Carol Price, who was born there and whose mother, my aunt, ran the hospital from 1953 to 1969. She told me about the information I could find at the Jackson County Historical Society

My pedicurist, Bethany Boyd, found the article on line about Pawnee Bill's son who died.

I am grateful for creative writing classes available to take online.

Other books to read are as follows:

The Girls Who Went Away by Ann Fessler
Fallen Women, Problem Girls by Regina G. Kunzel

THE WILLOWS MATERNITY SANITARIUM

THE WILLOWS MATERNITY SANITARIUM.

The location is ideal for its purpose. On a main thoroughfare of the city, but setting back over a hundred feet from the street and on a high terrace it offers seclusion and protection to its guests.

INTRODUCTION

This story of the beginning of my grandparents maternity hospital for unwed mothers to her end, since my aunt took over at that time, may be interesting to those who were patients at such a hospital, those who were born there and those who were children of the adoptees, and also history buffs of the early twentieth century. An early map shows railroads from all over the United States going to Kansas City, the baby hub of the United States. The stigma of pregnancy in the early 1900s was so embarrassing to families, even though the women were not taught anything about sex and didn't know what to expect when they were with a man.

My grandparents called them the Unfortunate Women. They wanted to give them the best care as if they were married and pregnant and in their own home town hospital. They didn't judge them nor condone what they did as some Kansas City officials accused them of. Grandmother, who took over the superintendent responsibilities when Granddad was ill and quit in 1928, was a mother of three, a son and two daughters. She was a super mom, commuting from home to hospital for many years. One of her daughter's, Lucille, was born crippled. She had to be taken care of by a nurse until Grandmother made an apartment at the hospital and had Lucille live with her after the other two children were grown and on their own. That way she didn't have to continue to pay a nurse to stay at the home on Summit Street.

My family lived in Kansas City with Granddad a few years during World War 11 and I often visited the hospital. I loved to go to the nursery and rock the babies in a swing if they were old enough. Grandmother made me a white nurses dress and gave me a white New Testament with Nurse printed on it which I still have. When we moved to Independence, Kansas I spent a few weeks with Grandmother each summer. My last summer was when I was eighteen and going to college that fall.

I have been gathering information for many years on The Willows Hospital and Sanitarium and now I'm ready to put it on paper. I hope those who read it, enjoy it and appreciate what this couple, my grandparents, went through trying to get the hospital started. I certainly do because I have started three businesses myself. I know how frightening it is to not know when business will pick up and when there are bills to pay.

All of the historic parts are true; the only fiction is about the girls who stayed there. Grandmother told me one of the girls reminded her of me. I got to meet her and when Grandmother said that, the patient said, "We are both blondes," but she touched her big stomach and said, "the resemblance ends here."

I took the liberty of copying forty-one pages of emails in 2005 from a Willows web site and have included those letters at the end. I hope it's not too late for some of those mothers and children to find the information for which they are looking. It is still very difficult to get birth mother records and birth certificates in most states. When bills are proposed in congress to allow that, they don't go very far. Some think if the mothers think they might lose their privacy, they might opt out for abortion instead. In this book you will see how important it was to guard the patient's identity.

You will read the letters from these families and see what different methods they used to try to find information about their biological parents.

My grandparents thought the greatest sufferer was the unwelcome child who was the innocent victim but was called bastard by many people.

The chapter titled "Priscilla" is about my daughter-in-law whose mother was born at The Willows. It is a delightful and inspiring story.

PART ONE

1905 TO 1930

CORA

One cold Christmas eve something shook me awake. Are we having an earthquake? I finally got an eye open to see it was my husband, EP, shaking me. "Cora, wake up" he yelled. "Nurse Ella said we have a fire somewhere in the house. We must get the babies and everyone else out. I'll get the babies and you get the mothers and patients. Ella will get the nurses." Once he saw I was awake, he ran out of our room.

Still groggy, I got up and tried to discern if the fire was coming from upstairs or down. I could smell smoke and feel heat as I went upstairs to wake the mothers. It was hotter up here and I knew heat rises so it must have been coming from below. The acrid smoke burned my lungs now and my eyes watered so badly I could barely see. Leaving my spectacles on the night stand didn't help.

I went into the first room while yelling, "Fire! Fire!" and woke one of the girls who hadn't yet delivered. I told her to get the others up and have them help others who had delivered and were too weak to run. I kept going, looking in each room and yelling to them to get up.

"Mrs. Haworth," Betsy, a patient, hollered. "What about the babies?"

"Mr. Haworth is getting the babies and Nurse Ella is getting the nurses." I was choking and didn't know from where my new found energy was coming. The crying babies were making the mothers frantic. "If the smoke is too heavy, crawl on the floor if you have to," I gasped. I lowered my self and crept downstairs. It seemed better there. I counted the girls as they came down, some backwards on hands and knees, all choking and wiping their eyes. A couple of the girls were so large with child, I was afraid this stress would cause them to go into labor. That was all we needed.

As Nurse Ella got the nurses up, I told them to help with the mothers who were weaker.

Neighbors helped EP carry out all nine babies. I watched them being taken to another house, an annex to the hospital. There were seven nurses and twenty patients. Everyone was saved, thanks to the firemen and neighbors.

I saw EP shivering as he led everyone to a cottage. I stood there too shocked to think of the cold as I watched our dream go up in smoke. And on Christmas Eve! I could now see that the fire was in the attic so that made it easier for us to get out. All I could think of was how hard we struggled to get The Willows Sanitarium established for unwed mothers. Why had God allowed this to happen?

I threw myself into EP's arms collapsing with exhaustion. "God spared us all," EP said. "Are your tears from the smoke?"

"No," I cried. "I'm thinking of our dream and the Christmas gifts to all the patients from their parents that are ruined."

"Our lives are our gifts for all of us are saved," EP answered.

"We also lost our clothes and their clothes we must replace," I said tearfully.

"We have insurance," EP calmly said trying to console me. "Let's go inside. The firemen will finish out here and give us a report. We have to find beds in the cottages for all these folks."

I told him I hoped they found out what caused the fire. It started in the attic. We had those extra mattresses there since we bought the Maddox home just ten days before.

EP for Edwin Pearl was Quaker born, Quaker bred and Quaker educated at Earlham College, a Quaker liberal arts college in Richmond, Indiana. I was twenty-seven and EP was twenty-eight when we married in 1903. We started the hospital in 1905. Our maternity sanitarium was only two years old and we needed an extra house to add to the other two cottages. The Maddox home was thirty-two years old and next to our bluff at 2929 Main Street in Kansas City, Missouri.

EP had been working since college and had saved quite a bit of money to buy the land on a bluff twenty feet high, a few blocks south of the Union Station, which made it convenient for the women to take the train from all points north, south, east and west to the hub of the United States. Pullman cars were plush passenger cars so travel was comfortable for those who could afford it. They had dining cars, hotel cars and sleepers and also refrigeration. And they traveled at forty miles an hour. Then, for only a few cents, the women could take a yellow cab to the hospital.

We spent the next two years planning how to build on with the insurance money we got from the fire. Edward Trickett, fire warden, had told us that upon investigation, the fire was started by excelsior-stuffed mattresses plus mice. How could mice start a fire I wondered? One day EP said he had some plans as he laid the outline before me. We were in the dining room downstairs where there was room on the large oak dining table to look at these plans. "For starters, let's build a breezeway connecting our three residences so we will be under one roof."

"That would be wonderful, especially in inclement weather but we need to be careful on expanding. We do have several acres but we want to be sure we don't rush things."

"I'm going to Maddox lumber yard to see what it will cost and how long it will take," he said as he pulled out his pocket watch to check the time.

Not only was EP Superintendent of the hospital but he also was a writer. His book, *Makin' Rhymes and Other Rhymes* was recently published. I didn't know how he found the time. Poetry just seemed to come naturally to him.

We decided to build this sanitarium because my little sister got pregnant and my family practically disowned her. It was such a stigma. Lila wasn't a bad girl, just an unfortunate one and the father was a no-account.

We lived in the small town of Mt. Vernon, Missouri where everyone knew everyone. My several brothers and sisters were not allowed to talk to Lila. We found out one of the townspeople was going to Illinois. My mother asked them if they would take Lila to visit some cousins who lived there. I worried so much about what was going to happen to sweet girls who succumbed to a man's charms. Sex was rarely discussed. If a girl missed her period, she didn't know why. I cried when Lila left and told her to write to me and tell me about our cousins. She was noticeably frightened but promised she would.

And, that's how I met EP. He was my third cousin, also a Haworth as we were. Lila liked him a lot. "He never judged me," she wrote in her childish handwriting. "I'm enjoying making baby clothes and embroidering them. I better not get too carried away until I know what it is."

For education, we girls were taught to embroider, sew, knit, crochet, needlepoint as well as read and write. I wondered what my family would do when Lila had her baby. She was only fourteen and I'm sure she would have liked to keep it and care for it like a little doll. Anyway she would not be able to come home with a baby.

It was a difficult time for all of the family, having to take sides but still wanting what was best for our sister and daughter's reputation.

Abortion was out of the question. Too many mothers died from having them.

CORA

Marketing and advertising were our most important jobs to get the word out and EP even wrote a booklet to doctors all over the United States called, *"Troubled Waters, Human Life According to Eastern Symbolism Is a Voyage Over Troubled Waters; The Sea Always Restless and Cruel; The Shore Quiet and Peaceful."*

EP wrote the following:

> *This book is addressed to the Medical Practitioner in the hope that it will aid him in bringing comfort and hope to his patient who may be voyaging upon a sea of torment far from the quiet, peaceful shore.*
>
> *Presume for a moment that you have a patient, the daughter of one of your best friends, a girl who has transgressed through weakness and not willfulness. In your search for the answers to her problem, there are many questions you wish answered.*
>
> *In this book we have tried to answer all of those questions you might wish to ask.*
>
> *We trust that you will read this book with pleasure to yourself and saving to the honor of the girl.*

I thought EP was so good with words. He also wrote *that after perusing this review, the doctor will not hesitate in recommending any good girl who has made the error of the flesh, to repair to The Willows for seclusion and protection. Any fear he or the patient's family might have of her being thrown among the undesirables and under demoralizing influences, will be dispelled by the words herein presented. Truly these are the ACCIDENTS OF SOCIETY. Accidents of Fair Travelers on the Highway of Life, published by The Willows Maternity Sanitarium, primarily for physicians, copyright 1918 by EP Haworth.*

> *The Willows Maternity Sanitarium is an institution devoted exclusively to the care and seclusion of unfortunate young women, offering them congenial, homelike surroundings before confinement and exceptional medical and hospital care during delivery and convalescence. In most cases, arrangements are also made for the finding of a home for the patient's baby for adoption.*
>
> *The institution will not knowingly accept a young woman of the immoral or degenerate type, its service being reserved for deserving young women who have made a misstep and who face social and moral ruin. The Willows' method is the safe, Christian and ethical solution to one of the most difficult problems of the medical community. The knowledge of use of preventatives and prophylactics by the promiscuous saves them from maternity hospital needs.*
>
> *Early entrance during gestation is important for preparing the patient for accoutrement through systematic hygienic methods and massage. A special system of abdominal and perineal massage have been originated for preventing persistent and severe vomiting and as an aid to labor.*
>
> *The abdominal markings of a single girl, caused by carrying a child, are telltale signs that might be discovered at a time and cause her misfortune to become known. This combination of massages, including the skin, perineal and vaginal massage, has been successful in sending numbers of girls, who have taken them, away from The Willows without marks or signs to show of their experience.*

A news article read,

> *Also, not just every unwed mother could get in. They were recommended by prominent doctors throughout the United States and not everyone qualified to adopt the babies. Some prominent entertainers were refused simply because they were in that ugly, dirty entertainment business.*
>
> *Qualifications for adoptive parents are high. The theory is that with nearly 100 applicants for every available baby, the agency can be choosy. Wealth is not a prerequisite, though the court requires that applicants offer proof of enough financial security to provide comfortable standards of living and education for the child. Also a couple who want a Kansas City baby must be regular church goers. Just belonging to a church isn't enough. After they heard from the adoptee's banker, doctor and clergyman, they had to have $38 to adopt a baby.*

We tried all sorts of marketing with our pamphlets to 16,700 doctors all over the country and advertising in the local Kansas City newspapers. We had no other choice. It wasn't just The Willows who adveriised. They included all the homes here too. So, EP and I were distraught, to say the least, over newspaper accounts from other towns questioning the legality of our advertising for parents to adopt our beautiful babies. For instance, what was wrong with this ad near Christmas?

"A MERRY CHRISTMAS. Why not brighten your home this Christmas by adopting an attractive, healthy boy? We have 30 boys of exceptional parentage ranging in age up to six months. For further information write or call personally. The Willows 2929 Main Street."

Or this one. "SAVE THAT BABY - AMERICA NEEDS IT. Twenty choice boys and girls for adoption, ranging in age up to 10 months. Call personally or write The Willows 2929 Main Street."

We had more requests for blond girls and during the Great War we were so crowded. Several local families let many of our patients stay with them until they were ready to give birth.

"This is the last straw, EP," I said. I was sitting at my desk in our office going through the day's mail. "We received a letter ordering us not to receive any more patients."

"Who is that from?" EP asked.

I was wringing my hands and started perspiring all over. I just couldn't believe it. Sometimes this stress was just too much.

"The Hospital and Health board," I answered. "They say we have an alleged disobedience to a ruling recently adopted by the children's bureau of the state board of health regarding the hospital to discontinue advertising babies for adoption. We have also been charged with failing to obtain permits from the state and city boards of health." I looked at EP. "Why didn't we know about this? This is the first I've heard of it."

When he didn't answer, I continued, "Listen to this article," I said.

> *Deceptive advertising circulated by maternity homes has made Kansas City a clearing house for nameless babies. Dr. R. E. Castelaw, superintendent of General Hospital, told the hospital and health board yesterday afternoon says the Kansas City Times.*
>
> *At least twenty-five girls reach the General Hospital each year, he said. As a direct result of this misleading advertising matter, they stay at a private maternity home until their funds are exhausted. In addition, most of them were furnished transportation home by the Provident Association.*
>
> *Doctor Castelaw's statement followed the reading of the investigative committee's report on the Willows Maternity Sanitarium, 2929 Main Street. That report, signed by Jacob Billikopf, Dr. Franklin E. Pearce and Mrs. E. W. Schaucler,*

> *accused the management of The Willows of deceiving its prospective patients. The hospital and health board has summoned DR. Edwin P. Haworth, its superintendent, to appear at the next meeting to answer to the charges.*

"You didn't tell me that," I cried. "But let me go on before I hear your excuses."

> *The report also censures a picture showing a large consulting staff of physicians and nurses, only one of whom admitted to the investigative reporter any work connected with being on the "staff." Several physicians did not know their names were being used.*
>
> *Sanitary conditions at The Willows, prices charged patients, the high infant mortality there and the management's lax attitude toward condoning morals and sins were criticized by the committee.*
>
> *Nine women, it stated, slept in one double room. Two slept in every bed as a general rule. The hospital and health board received the report on The Willows Sanitarium, the Fairmount Maternity Sanitarium, twenty first Street and Montgall Avenue and the Fairmount Maternity Sanitarium at 625 Arlington Ave. The recommendations in all three cases were the same. A resident physician of undoubted standing should be employed on salary and he should have no other financial connection with the sanitarium. A high class nurse should have charge of training schools. The pathologist from the general hospital should check soon the sterility of the operating rooms. The board also discussed the recommendation of the investigating committee that more should be exercised in allowing babies to be adopted from these maternity sanitariums.*

"Balderdash," EP said. He began pacing the floor. "They're crazy as a loon. They are talking about several hospitals. They can't be talking about just ours. Dr. Kepner is on salary and this is the only hospital in which he works. Mrs. Alice Dysart is head of the nursing school and no one could be more capable. Their pathologist is welcome anytime to check the sterility of our operating room." He stopped pacing for a moment and turned toward me.

" And where do they get off saying we don't have a large staff. We have ten nurses plus fourteen student nurses, housekeeper, cook, dining room girls, floor maids, private cook, engineer, porter and laundry helpers!"

He started pacing again. "And," he hotly continued, "we have plenty of room for our patients. I never heard of having so many sharing a room and a bed."

I couldn't remember ever seeing EP so angry.

He believed the local hospitals were losing money from births and were frightened.

"But we take care of the girls many months," I said, "which they can't do. So why are they against everything we do?"

I reminded him that when funds start running out for our patients, we put them in one of the cottages for less money. We have a nice apartment in one of the cottages we lived in before we bought our home on Summit Street.

The article continued, "*EP Haworth, proprietor of the institution, failed to appear before the board when he was asked to do so.*"

"Failed to appear before the board?" I exclaimed.

"I'll explain later Cora. Keep reading."

When he failed to appear, the board instructed Dr. Herman Pearse, city health director, to write him a letter telling him to stop taking patients until he obtained a city license and permit.

Mrs. C. M. James, head of the Veil and Women and Children's hospitals at 2001 East Eleventh Street, appeared before the court at its request today and said she would get her permit, which she had not done to date.

Mrs. James told the board she had not advertised babies for adoption since the new rule was adopted.

EP looked sheepish as he finally sat down and said, “I’m sorry I didn’t tell you Cora. I was asked to go before the board and I didn’t show up. They want us to stop taking patients until we get a license and permit. As a sanitarium, we didn’t have to report to the state. This is a new ruling. I’ve been going to do that but you know how busy we’ve been.”

“Well, I will go myself,” I said as I rose to my full five feet two inches. “We can’t stop taking patients. What were you thinking of?”

”No, I’ll go.”

“What if it’s too late? I remember when we doubled up women after the fire but not nine in a room! And that was two years ago. I need to find some aspirin.”

CORA

After the first six years, our employees consisted of the superintendent, assistant superintendent, office manager, secretary, cashier and bookkeeper, stenographer, obstetrician, pediatrician, superintendent of nurses, fourteen student nurses, housekeeper, cook, two dining room girls, floor maid, private cook for the superintendents, engineer, porter and two laundry helpers.

We secured financing and construction began on a new brick addition on the north side. Our hospital then had a capacity for caring for over fifty patients at one time. There were also accommodations for fifteen nurses and forty-five babies in the nursery.

Our training school had been open for four years. It started out as a twelve-month course for four years and the students got a moderate wage for their services. It was costing the hospital about $6000 a year which was a losing entity.

EP and I decided to lengthen the course to fourteen months and charge a small tuition. The new system allowed the student nurses to have a more complete knowledge of obstetrics and infant nursing and they would be recognized members of a profession excelled by few others.

In 1909 our new steam-heating plant and hot-water storage system was completed.

The first issue of The Willows Magazine appeared in 1911 and was issued bi-monthly and reached 16,700 physicians throughout the United States. It featured educational, inspirational and recreational subjects.

In late 1916 we made plans to erect another addition with two stories, a basement and a roof garden. With its completion there would be space for eighty-five patients and seventy-five to a hundred babies. This was timely as the Great War was in session which seemed to leave even more pregnant women without husbands.

The roof garden was designed with the idea of furnishing for the babies, a bright, airy and sunshiny room where they could enjoy a sun bath. It proved to be one of the coolest spots in the sanitarium for the nurses' summer use. From its windows one could see a beautiful view of surrounding parks and boulevards. A large tent was placed on the roof for shade and so the babies could get more air during the summer months. Water was run over the canopy for cooling.

Our hospital was the most modern with electricity and gas and up-to-date drinking fountains with ice-cold water on each floor. A loud speaker system connected all departments to make it possible to quickly summon any individual and to make announcements.

In the basement a fire-proof vault was equipped with modern metal files for all records.

In June of 1918 we were excited to see a total eclipse of the sun. We made sure all of the patients had the Sawtelle glasses, at ten cents each, in order to see the total eclipse. Many of the patients were hoping they would have a baby that day as a good omen. Others thought it might be bad luck. Scientists were excited about discovering new insights like proving Einstein's theory of relativity, which they did. The newspaper said the next total eclipse seen in the United States wouldn't be until 2017.

Because of the war, 1920 found the hospital at capacity. 1925 was our tenth anniversary and was a record-breaking year. We made plans to enlarge again. The number of employees had doubled in size.

We purchased a fifty-foot lot adjoining the hospital property on the south on the Walnut Street entrance to make space for a patient's park. We had it graded and fenced and planted shrubbery for a walking path around the perimeter.

EMILY

I was only twenty years of age in 1929 when I had to leave finishing school for The Willows Maternity Sanitarium. My mother and father made the arrangements. Mother said they chose the best for me. This institution was known as the Ritz or Waldorf in maternity homes. I had no idea how to compare it with others so I took mother's word for it.

When I stepped out of the yellow cab parked on Main Street, I looked up and saw lots of steps to the building on top of the bluff. I wasn't starting to protrude yet or else I wouldn't have been able to see the steps as I walked up. The brick building had a front portico that was attractive with vines climbing the columns and potted ferns on either side of the door. I looked back and could see the city in the distance that I would be a part of for six months. A nice-looking bespectacled woman with a wide smile answered the door. She was dressed like a nurse, all white dress and shoes. Her brown hair was in a pompadour.

"You must be Katrin. I'm Mrs. Haworth and I'm so glad to see you. Please come in to my office and we'll get you settled in no time. Is your luggage only one bag?"

"Yes, but I have all the required clothing packed in it."

"I love your hair cut," Mrs. Haworth said to me as we walked toward her office. "That is called Eton, is it not?"

"Yes," I answered. I was surprised she would take notice of fashion.

After checking her self in a nearby full-length mirror, Mrs. Haworth sat behind her elegant desk and asked me questions while she filled out the forms needed for my admittance. She also asked who the responsible party was, from then on referred to as RP. I didn't think that was anyone's business but she explained she needed his information so when it was time to find a family to adopt they would find someone with similar coloring, size and education. "What color of hair and eyes does he have?" she asked. She assumed I was ready to give up my baby.

I asked, "Do all the girls have to give up their babies for adoption?"

"No," she answered, " but I was under the impression you wanted to after visiting with your mother. What do you want to do?"

"Well, the RP as you call him, is a single teacher at the school I came from. He has brown hair and green eyes. He loves me and would marry me but after my parents came into an inheritance, I didn't think I would want to live with a poor man."

"You have six months to decide," she said. That made me feel better, in case I changed my mind. "I have you down for a double room. Is that right?"

"Yes, my mother said I have to share."

"Now, we give you a different name while you're here, for your protection. You will be Emily. Your mail will be addressed to Emily Haworth. Let me get Mrs. Maude Lowe, our administrator, to come for you and she will take you to your room and introduce you to some of the other patients. I know this can be a sad time for you so feel free to come to me with any problems. All right? At least your parents are accepting your condition."

I nodded. I felt a little overwhelmed.

As we left the office I heard the large music box on the hall tree playing a classical tune. I had never seen one so large. Mrs. Lowe said it played twelve tunes. It was a nice touch to hear in the background. It made the place feel less like a hospital, if not a home, at least a little less strange.

Mrs. Lowe took me to my room so I could hang up the clothing the hospital required me to bring: a housecoat, four smocks and six nighties. There were two narrow beds, two dressers, and one desk in my room. I had it to myself for the time being. The furniture was very dark wood and felt expensive as I ran my hand over it. A plush rug lay between the beds. The hallway of this wing had a window at the end, a nurses's desk in front of the window, chairs along the wall, and tables with games and magazines. I also noticed an upright piano along one wall. The flooring was linoleum in the hall.

"Let's go see more of the hospital and I'll introduce you to some other lovely women," Mrs. Lowe said as she directed me to follow. "We go through this door to the stairway that takes you downstairs to the dining room." She pushed open the door and glanced at me over her shoulder as I walked through it behind her. "You will meet lots of ladies at that time. But we will go past the stairs through another door and through a breezeway to the library." I could feel the difference in temperature in the breezeway. Mrs. Lowe explained to me that this breezeway is the way across the parking lot to the cottages. In the library she said, "We are affiliated with the Kansas City Public Library system so we keep up with the latest novels. Over here is a small shop that is open a couple of hours each day so you may purchase toilet articles as you need them. We even have some gifts and needlework. Do you have any questions?"

"Not yet," I said.

"Okay, outside this far door, down the hall to the right, back toward the front foyer is the phone you may use at anytime." I noticed we had made a loop. "You may stay up as long as you like, just don't disturb your room mate if she is sleeping."

"Tomorrow, if you want to see it, I'm sure one of the ladies will show you how to get to the park in back of the hospital. Some of the girls like to sit in the swing or walk on the pathway around the shrubs. It's very pleasant and private out there. They call it the bull pen for some reason. You really need to walk for exercise, you know."

She left me and I was eager to get my room fixed up. I had brought some decorative art to help me feel at home.

AUDREY

Mummy went with me by train from Tennessee to Kansas City to stay at The Willows. I was only fifteen. My blond hair was in a new bob which I could feel bouncing as I ran up the front steps in my jodhpurs and boots which were all I ever wore.

"Amy, slow down. You are carrying a child," Mummy said loudly. I was only two months pregnant so didn't show yet but Mum and Daddy were eager to get me out of our home and small town before I showed.

Mrs. Haworth greeted us with her very nice broad smile. I could tell she liked young people. She was so pleased to see us.

"Come in," she said. "Did you have a pleasant trip? Let's go into my office. My, you are such a cute little child. We will take good care of you."

I heard her bracelets jangle as she walked to her desk.

My Mum said, "She is used to her mammy doing things for her. I'm afraid she hasn't learned to do much for herself, but she is a good horsewoman. We have Tennessee Walking Horses and Amy rode every day. That is, until we found out she was pregnant. We don't know who the father is yet. She refuses to tell us."

Mrs. Haworth looked pensive. "Hmmmmm, we will have to do something to help occupy her time. We have a lovely park so she can be outside in nice weather any time she likes. We have games, a library, handiwork, and magazines. Do you know how to knit or crochet Amy?"

"No, not really. Do you have books on horses?"

"We get our books from the public library so I'm sure we can find something you will like. I'll have Mrs. Lowe take you to your room while I visit with your mother."

Mummy asked if she could see the room.

"I'm afraid not. This is a hospital of absolute seclusion. We give the girls a different name even, so no one will recognize them here. What name would you like to use Amy?"

"I always liked the name Audrey."

"Okay. You are Audrey Haworth. Your mail will be addressed to this address at that name. No one will ever find out your real name unless you tell them."

Mrs. Lowe took me down several halls to a wing that looked a bit dull. My roommate was Heather. She was a rather large girl and very plain looking with mousy brown hair. When I was shown around the hospital corridors, I noticed the back door downstairs by the dining room. A few minutes later I said I wanted to say goodbye to Mummy. Mrs. Lowe said she had probably left. Remembering where the back door was, I ran to the steps and down as fast as I could but had to wait for a very pregnant woman to go past. I then dashed out the door looking for a way around the building. I ran across the parking lot to the right but a fenced park was in the way. I ran back across the parking lot to the north side where I could get through. Mummy was almost to the steps to go down to get in the taxi.

"Mummy, wait," I cried, "do you have to go already?"

"Yes, dear, You will be fine. This is an excellent hospital. I will write to you. You may call me anytime."

We hugged and when I walked back in the front door, I got a small scolding from Mrs. Haworth for leaving like that.

"Mrs. Lowe didn't know where you were running to," she said. "Maybe your parents will visit some time. After all, you are going to be here a longer time than some others."

I went back to my room and met Heather, my roommate. I just wanted to cry but had to make nice.

HEATHER

"Hi, Audrey. I'm Heather Haworth. That goes well doesn't it? I feel like I've lost my identity though. Listen, I'm not into decorating. I'm just plain Jane. So, if you brought anything from home, feel free to hang it up or whatever. I will leave you and come back later so you will feel free to do what you wish."

"Do the Haworth's care if we hang pictures on the walls?"

"No, they want us to feel at home. We have our own dressers and we share a small closet since we don't have much to hang up. The girls here are very nice. Some are quiet at first but get more friendly as they get to know you. I'll take you to lunch and you will meet a lot of them there."

As I left, I heard some crying from our room. I knew she wanted to cry. Most of us did in such strange, sterile surroundings and also feeling we were abandoned, not only by the father of our baby but by our parents.

I went to the library for a while and when I returned, I saw that there were horse pictures on the walls and a rag horse on her bed. Audrey was just sitting there staring into space. She explained about why she liked horses. That's all she seemed to know.

"Audrey, let me show you the park. You will like being outside."

I took her through the breezeway to a back door, through Mrs. Haworth's tiny kitchen, through another door and to the park. We sat on one of the gliders. She spied the croquet set and seemed interested. "Do you want to play?" I asked.

She got up to go pick up a mallet and as we played, I had to shoot from the side because of my large stomach. She was able to put the mallet between her legs to shoot. "Audrey, when you get bigger, you can shoot like I do, from the side."

"I guess I'll have to," she replied.

After the game we went back inside and downstairs to the dining room for lunch. A calcium and iron pill were at each place setting. We could sit where we wished. I had Audrey sit with me at a table where two other really young girls sat.

"I'm surprised and pleased to see other young girls here," Audrey said.

Carol said, "Yes, these are the roaring twenties and I guess we took roaring a little too far."

I didn't think it was anything to laugh about. But then, I was forced upon.

Our soup and sandwich were brought to us and we ate in silence, which was difficult for Audrey.

"Audrey, do you have any questions?" I asked.

"What do y'all do around here? I'm going to be here a long time. I'm already homesick for my mammy."

"And not your parents?" Carol asked.

"My mammy always took care of me and did everything for me. She even dressed me."

"It isn't hard to dress when all we wear are smocks," someone said.

"It takes awhile to get used to all the newness but we find games to play, magazines and books to read and help do manicures and pedicures if we want. It's hard to bend over for pedicures. We also knit and crochet. We teach each other if someone doesn't know how. Do you want to learn something like that?"

"I don't think so. What if we need a haircut?"

"Usually we can find someone to cut our hair. We don't have to be fashionable. We rarely go anywhere, but if you want to, you can get an appointment at a hair salon and take a cab."

"And, if you need a gift for someone, a knit or crocheted gift would be nice and we can buy the materials in the gift shop."

"You can talk to any of us about anything. We need to get stuff off our chests and it won't go any further than here," Carol said.

CORA

EP and I lived in one of the cottages until we started our family. I was pleasingly plump I preferred to think and I wore my brown hair in a pompadour. My uniform was a white starched dress like my nurses wore but mine was fancier with tiny front pleats that my ironing lady complained about constantly. I was always adjusting my spectacles and my bracelets clanged as I walked the hall ways. EP said everyone knew when I was coming.

EP was six feet two inches tall with dark neck-length hair and he was quite handsome. He had a grace about him, soft spoken and usually calm, unless he was punishing one of our children by using his thumb to thump the top of their head. I was more animated when I talked, more nervous about things being done correctly and I thought I was very pretty at times, depending on the hair and fashion trends and I made sure I was always up to date.

EP and I were working in the office when the phone rang. I picked it up and listened. EP saw me put it down in shock.

"What's the matter?" he asked. "You look like you've seen a ghost."

"I don't know whether to cry or yell or keep silent. I am horrified that I may get some other such calls."

EP got me a glass of water and gently urged me to tell him what the call was about.

I looked at him sadly and said, "One of the girls' father called that he was going to put his daughter in another home because we have crowded them so much. What if others call and say the same? We can't afford to lose them EP. He must have read one of the Kansas City articles reporters often write to complain about maternity hospital conditions. I think our general hospitals put them up to that."

"Yes, we have had to double them up in rooms and put some in the hall ways, but very seldom. They are getting the best of care. What other hospital gives them massages and spa baths? They won't want to go to another hospital. Let's wait and see what that father's daughter says when he talks to her about that."

EP always made me feel better. His demeanor was always slow, soft and mellow compared to mine. He never seemed to worry but I worried enough for the two of us.

I was so grateful to him for wanting to start a hospital for unwed mothers. Thanks to my sister, Lila, something was being done to help other unfortunate women. Lila was back in Mt. Vernon where she found a nice man to marry. The people of Mt. Vernon were told only that Lila went away to visit relatives and help care for a sick cousin. Luckily for her, a childless couple who lived near where she was staying in Illinois fell in love with Lila's daughter and adopted her. Lila didn't like having to make the decision to give her up but she knew it was best for her child. And she knew she could now go back home to her once loving family. It was a difficult time for all of them, having to take sides but still wanting what was best for Lila's reputation.

AUDREY

It wasn't a very lively place, of course. The others were further along than I was. I had too much pep. I wanted things to happen. I wondered if I could get a betting game going? I went to see what they had.

I wondered how my horse trainer was doing with my horses. Lawsy me, I wondered how he was doing without me? I couldn't let my parents know who gave me this baby. They would fire him for sure.

I really missed my mammy. She did everything for me. Here I was expected to keep my bed made and my laundry done. I was even asked if I wanted a job in the laundry for pay. Of course I didn't want to work. I'd never have to work. My work was showing my horses and I loved that so it wasn't work for me.

One day Heather came in and seemed upset. "What's wrong?" I asked.

"I wish you would pick up your clothes off the floor," she said angrily. "It's hazardous trying to get around in here. What if someone falls and miscarries?"

"Sorry. I'm used to my mammy picking them up. I'll try to do better," I said hanging my head in shame.

"Some of the girls are coming in to listen to the radio and gab. We need to make room."

Four girls came in and sat down or lay down on our beds. They started gabbing and I had to join in or leave the room. That's why I didn't like sharing a room.

When they started singing along with a song that was on the radio, I noticed what a lovely voice Heather had. "Heather!" I said with awe. "You have a beautiful voice. Did you take professional lessons?"

"I just sang in the church choir," she said.

"Let's see how many here have talent like that and we can have a talent show. Wouldn't that be fun? And you should sing in the dining room before we eat."

"I would have to sing without accompaniment down there. The piano is up here."

I could see that Heather was pleased someone noticed her voice.

I wanted to get the others thinking about this. "Surely someone plays the piano and probably others play instruments," I resumed.

Mable spoke up about who played piano in her wing and someone who played violin.

"I'll go to the other wing and find out what talent is hiding there," I said. "This will be tremendous."

Emily came in and asked what the excitement was all about. She was the most educated and beautiful. After all, she was a college girl.

"We're going to have a talent show or contest," I said excitedly. "I'm going to go to each wing and find out what talent is hiding there."

"They would have to practice songs," said Emily. "What if some aren't as good at reading music as others? What if they don't want to compete? Some people like to compete but some don't."

Heather piped up, "Oh, don't be a killjoy Emily. They don't have to compete if it's just a musical show. I'm sure we can find a few to try out. I know I can make it happen if Audrey finds out who will join us."

CORA

EP got the license and permit but he hadn't been feeling well. I knew he wanted to write. He had had two poetry books published and he wrote *Nitro by Hypo*, which was a book for the doctors. In fact he covered everything of which a small sampling follows:

- *Surgery has been performing miracles not conceived of since the days of Christ. Drugs, compounds and concentrates have revolutionized medical treatment. Radium has showered blessings on mankind. Mechanical, electric and hydro-therapeutical means have been invented in the treatment of countless maladies. Vaccines and serums are employed in battle with myriad of germs that are gnawing at mens vitals. And what are you doing? Are you keeping up with the times?*
- *The physician gives of life and to life. He adds days to days and prolongs man's time for enjoyment. His gift is to humanity. Then why should not such pay, as he may receive in the coin of the realm, coming from such abundance and being of such comparative insignificance in value, be generous indeed.*

- *Make it your business to read medicine daily. You must keep up with the latest.*
- *As for religion, the doctor should have Faith to endure hardships, brave the dangers of the tortuous elements, face the ravages of contagion and pestilence, even defy, then succumb to the conqueror, Death, in the interest of humanity.*
- *Before you start out on this trip, waste five minutes. Go back to your office, take down your latest book treating the disease you are fighting and see if there isn't some new point to gain in the management of the case. A few moments spent every day in the study of your severe cases is the best spent time you have.*
- *A doctor preaches health, sunshine, exercise etc. But he leads the most abominable life. His exercise is bouncing along in a buggy in the fresh air or in his car going from patient to patient. Thirty minutes with a tennis racket in hand and old Sol baking the poison out of his body through the ruddying skin, will however not only add to his physical powers but give him clearer brain cells for diagnosing diseases and scribbling prescriptions.*
- *What is your income per year? Supposing your annual income to be $2,000. Set aside at least five per cent for new apparatus, drugs and medicines plus books and journals.*
- *Be sure to use the Golden Rule. Ethics, ethics, ethics are so important.*
- *Think of the nurse's burden. She has a pretty hard lot and has to go home and take care of the family. Can you do anything to relieve the nervous tension under which she is laboring to save your patient?*
- *Always be cheerful and buoyant. Your patient's confidence in you is the real battle.*

There were many chapters and pages to help the doctors. EP was so thoughtful and had such a moral background.

EMILY

I was trying not to feel homesick. There were lots of girls here to visit. I didn't know how easy it was for them to talk about themselves. Pregnancy was never talked about in polite society but I was curious who everyone's RP was. I decided to call Mother to let her know how I was being absorbed into this atmosphere.

"Hi mother, it's me."

"Oh, honey, I'm so glad you called. I'm having a terrible time with the servants. Not really terrible, but I just don't know how to handle them. That's why we sent you to that finishing school so you could learn all the niceties and teach us, but you didn't FINISH."

"What's the problem with them?"

"I keep telling them what to do and they act like they don't care."

I sighed. "How do you approach them?"

"I often have to yell at them. I want the cook to buy groceries for me and prepare the meals ***I*** want. I want the yard man to plant certain kinds of plants and he tells me they won't grow here."

I took a deep breath. I thought Mother would be more curious about me. "So, Mother, you are not to be bossy to them. Sure, you are above them in status but you have to show respect for them. Just be assertive, not aggressive. As for the yard man, go out in the yard with him and tell him why you want certain plants and ask him what would grow there in colors you would like."

"Okay dear. I will try that. How is The Willows treating you?"

"People are very nice here. There is no judgment. They want to do all they can for us to have an easy pregnancy. They make sure we take our pills like calcium and iron. The pills are in front of our plates in the dining room. They even give us periodic massages so we won't have scars after giving birth."

"Well, call again when you can. We aren't allowed to call you because they don't really know it's us in case someone wants to know if you are there and say it's us. They are very strict about seclusion for you."

"Bye, now. I'll call you in a few days. I hope you get along better with the servants. Is Daddy doing well with them?"

"He doesn't know how to handle them either. Ever since he got his inheritance, he's not sure how to handle it. I hope he doesn't spend it foolishly and lose it. I love you."

AUDREY AND CORA

I ambled in to my room in a tizzy to find Heather sprawling on the bed listening to Kansas City's Charlie Parker on the radio.

"Heather, have you heard the scandal pertaining to this sanitarium? I called mummy and she read it to me from the newspaper."

"What happened?" Heather jumped up to ask me.

"A famous opera singer adopted a baby from here just to deceive her divorced husband. If she could prove she was pregnant when he left her, she would get more money."

"How would she be able to adopt a baby with that background? The Haworth's were very particular who adopts their babies, so we've been told."

"I don't know. I hope we find out." I decided to rest also and listen to the music.

I also saw the newspaper article and invited my three employees who were also my friends into the office. EP was also coming over with another article but it was raining again. He would be late if the street cars were slow.

"Have you seen these New York newspaper headlines?" I asked.

"The gossip is already going around the halls," Mrs. Dysart said.

"Well, of course. It's been in all the papers and I'm sure our patients are talking to their parents. We don't need this kind of publicity," I emphasized.

One headline, in big bold type, read,

BORROWED CHILD TO GET ALIMONY.

Another read,

BORROWS BABY TO PLOT TO DECEIVE.

"Land sakes. I am just appalled that someone would use us for that purpose," I said. I plopped into my chair behind my desk. "How could this have happened? Mrs. McKwen, you are the head of the adoption department. Do you know who this woman is?"

Mrs. McKwen said, "I'll have to look into all the paperwork to see. It was a fraud to be sure. You know we have to have references from the family doctor, a clergyman and a banker?"

Mrs. Lowe, who was bookkeeper said, "I don't know of anyone with the name of Lydia Locke Marks, who apparently is a concert singer."

Mrs. McKwen brightened up as she said, "I do remember a woman who wanted an older baby. Maybe that was because she had to prove she was with child before she divorced her husband."

"EP is here. Let's ask him what we should do, if anything."

EP took off his galoshes and rain coat after he retrieved the newspaper out of his coat pocket. He set his umbrella in the stand and took a seat. He looked exhausted, I thought. The weather had been so damp for days. Kansas City had so much rain and even floods lately. But he said he wanted to come.

He unfolded the paper and read the columns as here stated.

Former Singer Accused of Taking Baby from Orphanage to Get $300,000.

A little child led Mrs. Lydia Locke Marks, former opera singer, into court today. She had intended that it should lead her to the tidy sum of $300,000 provided for such an emergency by her ex-husband.

She had apparently adopted the child under a false name and represented it as her own, according to evidence, in order to claim the large sum held by her divorced spouse for her in case there should be a child.

At the time of her divorce from Arthur Hudson Marks, wealthy manufacturer, last September, a settlement of $100,000 was made on the wife and the promise of $300,000 more in case a child was born to her, it was brought out.

Mrs. Marks appeared at The Willows Hospital calling herself Mrs. Ira Johnson of Hannibal, Missouri

Mrs. McKwen jumped in and said, "I remember that name."

"Let me finish this article."

and equipped with references which presumably satisfied institution officials of her financial and social responsibility for the adoption of a child. Papers were drawn up but not signed.

Later, at her sister's home, she obtained a birth certificate from the family physician, naming the baby boy Arthur Hudson Marks, Jr.

She came with the child and little Arthur, otherwise Irving Harvey, thrived in his baby way. He looked about him in the big court room today and kicked his red heels out of the blankets. And nobody knew whether he was glad to be given back to the hospital or not. At least Arthur had one thrilling adventure.

"Well," I said, as I sat back in my chair. "I wonder what will happen to that baby boy?"

"They are going to send him back if I read that correctly," EP said. "This was a fraud. The only good news about this is that some wealthy people used our hospital to adopt a baby so we have to look on it that sometimes bad news is good news as it gets advertising."

"Another article said that Orville Harold, an opera tenor, hired a detective to find out where and when she had that baby. He found out he came from here."

Mrs. McKwen said, "We should be more careful with the references. What did she say about a husband? We always want a husband and father. Someone was careless."

I stood up and dismissed the ladies saying, "We're not going to do any judging right now. We must re-adopt the "borrowed" child and hope the future parents don't know about this. We will have to explain why he's so old though."

"Stay for dinner EP and we'll drive home together. I'm so tired of this rain. The girls can't go out to the park and it is getting on all of our nerves."

EP agreed with me but said, "Emery Byrd, Thayer is having a sale on ARDOC coats. I may get one myself. They are advertised as a coat that can be worn five different ways; an Auto coat, Rain coat, Dress coat, Opera coat and for all occasions."

I asked him if that was only for today. He said, "Of course. They want business on a rainy day."

"You take the car then and come right back and be careful driving in this rain."

I thought, darn advertising. But if you are in business, you have to do everything you can to get it.

EMILY

I was glad we were finally getting into a routine. There really wasn't much to do. I sat in my room a lot and looked at the wall paper with tiny designs. I counted how many designs were in a certain space. How boring is that? I had already read the Ladies Home Journal, Harpers Bazaar, Vogue and Life magazines on the hall table. I almost wished I had a roommate, but surely it would't be long with so many coming in daily. Every night I heard crying, mostly from new girls. Some had reasons to cry, like if their parents disowned them. They wouldn't even take their daughter's phone calls. Some girls missed their RP's. Some RP's even visited them.

Audrey was so young and was always wanting someone to "play" with her. She liked action games and loved croquet in the bull pen. And then she wanted to have a talent show.

I called my mother rather often but tried to give more space to that. I read books from the library. Some of the girls liked to talk about what they read which encouraged others to read the same book. We thought of starting a book club. Audrey loved to start things. I decided to give her that idea and then I could work on the details. However, she wanted to read books only about horses.

I started feeling some movement which was exciting. Really, I didn't know what to expect. No one seemed to know anything and we were all learning daily and then talking about it so others could gain from our experience. We never got the chance to talk to the patient after she became a mother. She was kept on another floor and left in ten days. Occasionally we would hear a rumor of a baby who didn't make it or a caesarian birth. One of the girls had a bad hip that the doctor repaired.

Evenings at candle-lighting time we tended to gather in Heather's room to visit. Someone had sneaked in Saratoga chips so we munched loudly. As we got to know one another, we divulged more about ourselves and our situations. Heather was so loud, the others were afraid she would blurt out what they were sharing and others would hear. Not that it would go anywhere.

Last night Audrey told us about her love affair with her horse trainer. He was four years older and very good-looking she thought. He lived at a neighboring ranch and knew so much about horses, he could handle any of them with firmness and grace.

He had shown Audrey how to lead a horse into the arena and show him off so all eyes were on the horse and not on her.

"We made love in the horse trailer," Audrey laughed, "because when it rocked, one would think it was the horses moving. No one would walk in on us there."

Someone said, "Don't come knockin' when the horse trailer's rockin.'

We all laughed. She really was so cute. She couldn't wear jodhpurs any longer. We were all in smocks of some kind and color. And as our stomachs got bigger, the smocks got shorter in front — not very attractive. But no one really saw them.

The stores downtown were advertising maternity dresses that were so much more attractive than our smocks. They were loose-fitting with drop waistlines and reached just below the knees. Some dresses were wrap arounds. I guess if we were going anywhere to be seen, I would've wanted to wear one of those.

I told them about my school teacher, how kind he was and that he really did love me but I didn't think he could afford me since my now highfalutin parents had come into some money. "I'm getting use to fine things," I said.

"Yeah, like the Waldorf of maternity homes," Audrey piped up. That started everyone giggling.

"So, my parents have struggled all their lives and I don't want to have to do that," I said as I was lounging in a chair.

Heather pushed her brown hair back and rolled her eyes. "Were your parents happy though? All my Father does is work and worry about the stock market. I can't see that my parents are happy at all. Mother hardly sees Father unless they are entertaining his clients. They spend lots of money on clothes but I don't see that it makes them happy. I would love to be loved by a daddy. I wonder how we are going to look back on these months. I hope I forget as time goes on."

Audrey looked at me and whispered, "But it could be a happy time for you if you married your professor and kept your baby."

I piped up with, "Do you think we will think about our child the rest of our lives? I know I'll be praying for mine. How can I let him know I gave him away out of love?"

"Mrs. Haworth said the adoptive parents are so thrilled to have a baby since the woman couldn't conceive. That's a nice thought, don't you think?" Audrey asked.

Heather said, "I have a friend who had an abortion and she always feels so guilty. I will probably feel guilty giving mine up."

But not so much as having it killed, I thought. But I'll always wonder where he or she is and if he's happy.

HEATHER

I still had a couple of months to go when a thought came into my mind as I lay on my bed: I sure hoped this baby looked like his father. I didn't want it to go through life being judged as homely. I hoped labor was not too painful. I couldn't stand pain. Mother said I'd always had a low threshold of pain. Thank goodness I could be put out so I didn't feel it. I wished she had told me more about birth. After all she had gone through it several times. She never talked about sex either. So, how could they blame me for what happened?

What if I died? Some women died at child birth. Would my parents miss me or be glad they were rid of me? What would they have told their friends of how I died?

My massage nurse told me not to worry. It was a happy pain. And with all the care we got here at The Willows, like keeping us on a low caloric diet so we didn't gain too much and the regular massages so our skin would not show stretch marks and so at birthing time we would feel relaxed.

I knew it was a good place to be under the circumstances but I sure missed home. Even the wall paper in my room reminded me of home with pretty rose buds and a blue background. And so did the lace curtains. Mrs. Haworth took care in the furnishings so we would feel at home. She said, "Nothing but the best for my girls."

Mrs. Haworth called the father's the "responsible party" whereas one of the other homes called them "betrayer." I thought Mrs. Haworth showed more class. And she didn't make us feel shamed like my parents did. They didn't want to have anything more to do with me. At some other homes, they thought the mother-to-be was feeble-minded or sexually delinquent.

I'd no idea what my date would do when I left my girl's school for a weekend to attend a dance at a military academy in a nearby town. Several of us from our school went. One of my mother's friends fixed me up with a blind date. I sure got in a fix. I was the one who turned out to be blind. He had a flask in his pocket from which he drank. He was polite to offer me some but I didn't even like the smell of it. I was a big girl but he over powered me. It sure wasn't voluntary on my part. If I had told my father who he was, he would have killed the boy. He probably wouldn't have believed me anyway. It wasn't anything I enjoyed, especially not with his whiskey breath on me. Mother knew who it was but she wouldn't tell Father either for fear of what he would do. I couldn't believe this happened to me, a Christian girl who sang in the church choir!

The Haworth's told us not to dance close since that was what caused this to happen. Dancing didn't bother me. I wondered why it caused the boy to do that to me? If that was what couples had to go through to have babies, I didn't think I wanted to be married.

CORA

EP took me by the hand, into the living room at home and sat me on the floral chintz davenport to tell me what he had on his mind.

"Cora dear, you know I haven't been feeling well. Maybe I caught something when I went to Europe but the doctors don't know why I'm so fatigued. Maybe it's because I run the hospital and also write, which I prefer to do. You know, as a Quaker, we encourage women to lead. You have done a magnificent job with the patients and staff. You have been my right hand. We commute to our home here on Summit Street twice a day. I would like to stay here and oversee the nurse who takes care of Lucille, Ruthie and Donald. I can have more time to write."

I wasn't surprised. Poor Lucille was born crippled and I hated to leave her with her little crutches each day but a woman was needed at the hospital to oversee the patients.

"You know, Cora, if you need any help at all, I will come over to help, don't you?"

EP looked so sad. His face sorta hung.

"Of course. I know that. I've seen this coming and I'm so glad you trust me to do the superintendent's job."

EP continued, "We have faced many challenges together and we will have more I'm sure. Remember the fire shortly after we opened and the license and permit I didn't know we had to have and our attempt to get patients by advertising and marketing? Well, we can still market with our magazine but we had to stop advertising the way we did in the newspapers."

"What about the car?" I asked. We had just bought another Cadillac and if I took that to work, what would he do?

"The street car goes right in front of our house. I can take that. You take the car."

So, we had another change to get used to. For dinner I usually brought food from the hospital kitchen home to the family so I didn't have to cook. I took time to visit the children before their bed time. Our son Donald was seven years older than his sister, Ruth, and she was a year older than their sister, Lucille. Don was able to help out a lot.

Norman School, where they attended, was just two blocks away. Normally Ruth and Donald would walk but our nurse drove Lucille to school.

CORA

Kansas City was called Paris of the Plains. I guess because it was a highfalutin town. It grew fast and by 1900 had a population of almost 200,000. It had witnessed several Civil War fights that were all won by the Confederates. My father had been in the Civil War. A full-page article was written up about him in the Kansas City paper.

We owned a large concrete-block three story home on Summit Street, valued at $11,000. The average home at that time was $6,000. We and the Hyles, who lived next door, had similar homes. Other homes on the block were smaller and stuccoed and mostly were rented for up to $65 a month.

We needed a large home for a nurse to live in with the three children. EP and I used the largest bedroom with the single bath across the hall. One time poor Ruthie fell in front of one of the glass-doored book cases in the house and cut her knee rather badly. We had to take her to have stitches.

The nurse had the third floor which consisted of two bedrooms and a bath. Lucille slept in the second bedroom there so the nurse could help her get ready for bed and get up in the morning.

There were three bedrooms on the second floor.

Our home had beveled windows, a large foyer with a hall tree to hang coats and hats and a bench that had a seat that lifted up for galoshes and umbrellas.

There was also a living room, library and dining room. The kitchen had an ice box so an ice man came daily to add a block of ice to keep the food cool. A milk man left quarts of milk at the front door. Rocco, the trash man, came twice a week to pick up the trash and garbage. He also did the same at the hospital. I felt sorry for him having to be with that stinking, and I mean stinking garbage all day but he was the friendliest man and loved the children.

A coal furnace was in the basement and there was plenty of room for Ruthie and Don to roller skate in bad weather.

The garage in back was also made of concrete blocks and had an upstairs where union soldiers had stayed during the war with an opening in the floor to push down hay for their mounts below. It now held a Cadillac.

CORA

There were seven maternity homes for unwed mothers in Kansas City at one time and we took pride in The Willows being able to offer the most modern in heating, cold water in each room and giving massage for the patients to help them not end up with scars so they could keep their secret longer. We were also a hospital. The maternity homes took their patients to a hospital for birth. We encouraged exercise, and attendance at the weekly church service held in the library. Being so close to downtown, the girls could take a taxi and go shopping or to the movies. They were not kept in a prison.

Each State Board of Control had to approve the hospital before a couple from that state could adopt.

The Willows had some problems with the state of Minnesota in 1930. We received a letter from the board because the state did not approve of our method for carrying for illegitimate children.

I read their letter with interest, especially where they insisted that a child should be breast fed by its mother for at least three months, whereas The Willows separated the mother and child in ten days.

Minnesota also thought that our care tended to breed repeaters if the girls could extricate themselves from the predicament so easily.

Minnesota also believed that some of our girls were known to be of rather low mental capacity. So how could The Willows say their babies were exceptional in physical and mental qualities?

The letter ended with,

> *Altho such an institution may afford an opportunity for women and girls to hide from public view and summarily leave their children, it does not appear to the Board of Control of Minnesota that such a program promotes standards and really affords the most favorable outlet for the unfortunate illegitimate child.*

I immediately called in my assistant, Mrs. Lowe, to take dictation for a return letter. Mrs. Lowe had been on staff since the beginning so I felt she could give suggestions to help if needed.

"You know being sent to The Willows gives a young lady the opportunity to see the source of all the women's weakness while here. Others may likewise see in her peculiarities of personality and temperament, of education and environment that have influenced her life. Each of our girls is receiving her education and expanding her outlook on life. She's getting prepared for the problems the future has for her."

"Yes, Mrs. Haworth. One girl is perhaps permitted too much latitude with her men company or maybe is allowed or even encouraged to keep company with young men before she is old enough to control herself or to know the significance of certain unmanly actions."

"I always thought a woman needs constant vigilance by her mother much of the time. To be unchaperoned is to invite disaster," I said. "EP always said, dancing is one of the most serious causes of the sexual error with young men and women today. For them to be wrapped in each others arms and moving in perfect unison of rhythmic vibration to each other under the influence of the voluptuous waltz and jazz music of today, induces sexual excitement. If others weren't around, the intimate physical embrace becomes a mere inflation and training for the same intimate contact in private."

"That sounds like Mr. Haworth," Mrs. Lowe said.

"Well, enough of that, let's get on to the letter I want you to send."

"But, how many mothers even tell their daughters about sex? I have a son and I hope his father tells him something."

I sent the following letter to Minnesota.

Dear Mrs. Denter,

We have your letter of February 9 and we know that you must be quite upset over the information given to you by the welfare worker.

Perhaps you will be better satisfied if you write to Dr. Hubbard of Manhattan since he furnished one of your reference letters and ask his opinion as to our institution and its reputation for we are sure that he will give you his candid opinion.

As for the welfare worker, the Minnesota Children's Bureau does not approve of people living in the same state of Minnesota going outside of the state to adopt a child. They feel that you should adopt one from some Minnesota Home. Furthermore, they believe that patients who give birth to illegitimate babies should keep them and nurse them for at least three months. We believe that the baby, as well as its mother, is best served by the mother of the child releasing it for adoption. In this way it is given a name and its mother has another chance to make something of her life. Our methods are just opposite that of most welfare organizations for we feel that we care for different types of patients than are found in charitable organizations. Since our home is not a charity institution, we require our patients to pay for their period of seclusion and our patients are girls from good middle class homes who have made a socio-moral error. They are ordinarily with us from two to three months previous to their confinement and as we have daily contact with them, we are in position to know much about the patients' back ground. Our patients are nearly all sent to us by their family physicians and they are from small towns and the country.

All of our patients are examined upon entrance and this includes a Wassermann test. We take three histories while a patient is in our institution and we furnish the foster parents with all information except the home address of the mother of the baby. In no instance do the patients know where their babies are placed nor by whom they are adopted.

All of our babies are examined by a baby specialist when they are ten days old and we keep no defective babies nor do we offer such a child for adoption. The Willows Album being sent to you under separate cover will no doubt enlighten you on The Willows' methods and on the institution itself.

We are sorry that you have become so upset over this matter, but as we happen to know that the welfare workers tell like stories to all Minnesota applicants who apply to our institution for babies, we think little about it as we are used to it. It does not influence these people who really want a baby from our institution and are willing to wait until we can supply them with a suitable child. Under the Missouri law, foster parents are protected against three diseases when due to prenatal influence or ferocity up to the time a child is five years old, namely syphilis, feeblemindedness and epilepsy. Should foster parents adopt such a child, they may return it to the institution from where they adopted it, and they have no further obligation. Before the option decree becomes final, foster parents are given a 90 days probationary period.

Trusting that this explanation answers your questions satisfactorily, I am

Very truly yours,
Cora M. Haworth, Supt. The Willows

(I also sent a list of twelve sets of parents from Minnesota who wished to adopt and only half were approved for adoption. Others were disapproved or abandoned the application from the Minnesota Children's Bureau)

Letters went back and forth for five years.

CORA

"It's good to see you EP. Let me take your coat and hat." I loved greeting EP because he usually greeted me when I got home.

"How are you doing dear? I wrote a new poem just for you. Do you have time for me to read it to you?"

He sat down on the davenport and laid his cane beside him. He always carried a cane now but mostly it was hanging over his arm.

"Of course, I'm eager to hear it," I said as I sat beside him and glanced at the clock.

"This is for my book, *Sunshine and Roses.* It's called *If I could Sit By You,* which I'm doing now" he said sweetly.

If I could sit by you, my love,
If I could sit by you,
And hear your tender words, sweet love,
In accents old, yet new,
If I could sit by you and hear,
Through all eternity,

Your silver sigh, "I love you, dear,"
Would be too short for me.

"That's beautiful dear," I said and I gave him a hug. "I'm glad you have time to work on your poetry you love so much."

"I'm thinking of starting a novel too. The character's name is Scarlett and it will be a love story."

I thought, always the romantic. "That's quite an unusual name. How did you pick that for your heroine?"

"I know how women blush so easily so some of their faces get rather scarlet."

He continued with another subject. "Our son, Don, came home from school laughing at the girls who wore such big hats, they couldn't fit them into their lockers so they had to put them on top. He said the hallways looked like a millinery shop."

"He's such a nice young man, Cora. We are so lucky to have our three children. Poor little Lucille wants to walk and run and she has to use those little crutches. The nurse is real good with her though. When we go places, we use the wheel chair so the nurse and I can wheel her faster to keep up with the children."

I asked, "Did you take the pay-as-you-go car to get here?"

"Yes," He laughed. "The conductor said people don't seem to mind paying a fare now to take the street car."

"EP, I've been meaning to ask you about what to do when these girls want to smoke cigarettes. They are so popular now. Everyone does it."

"Everyone smokes but us, Cora. But we must be fair with them. I would say they can smoke in their room if they have a single room. But if they have a roommate who doesn't smoke, I would ask her to smoke outside in the park. Maybe if it's too hot or cold out, they will quit. It's a smelly habit, I think."

EMILY

I had some food for thought after listening to the girls talk about their parents' happiness. Most of them had money. If Daddy hadn't gotten his inheritance I wouldn't have been able to go to that nice college where I met Mel.

I wondered if Mel wanted me to get pregnant so I would have to marry him. No, I didn't think he was like that. I'd like to finish school but if I agreed to marry him and with a child, I don't see how I could finish school.

I'd been working in the nursery on the roof and just loved those little ones. They were so vulnerable and needed so much care and I loved caring for them.

Mel wanted me to keep the baby but I just couldn't unless I married him. He was my first love. Oh, I dated before but not like that. He really was very sweet and smart. I just hadn't had a chance to explore.

My parents were afraid of having a large wedding for me since they were not yet in with the local crowd. But if I kept the baby, they wouldn't have to have a big wedding. They would've wanted me to keep it as quiet as possible. I could put the baby up for adoption, go back to school and then marry Mel. I wondered how he would feel about that? I thought about one of the girls who had recently done just that. She was so excited about going home to a wedding without a baby.

I wished I could sleep. I kept pondering over my dilemma. I decided I would call Mel on the weekend. He had written me but I hadn't answered. And I was tired of losing sleep over it.

"Hi Mel, it's me," I said hesitatingly. I was calling from the front foyer of the hospital, near the office and I hoped no one could hear me.

"Hi, darling. It's so nice to hear your sweet voice. You haven't answered my letters so I was afraid I wouldn't hear from you again. Are you doing okay?"

My knees were weak just hearing his voice. I shouldn't have called him. I quickly hung up. I ran to my room and crashed on the bed, tears streaming down my cheeks, ruining my makeup. Why couldn't I make up my mind? I had too many options, unlike many of the other girls in here. I just couldn't handle a husband and baby right now. I wanted to finish school. I couldn't see how it was possible. I had to go down to dinner and I looked horrible.

I washed my face and put my makeup back on. After all, I was known for my bright look. But I wasn't fooling anyone. When I sat with my friends, Heather noticed I didn't look happy.

"What's your problem?" she asked me.

"Oh, I just called my professor friend at school and when he answered I hung up on him."

"But why would you do that?" Audrey asked.

"I didn't remember how sweet he sounded and I got cold feet. I want to finish school so I don't think I can keep the baby even if I married him."

Heather said I was lucky to have a loving man who wanted to marry me and would probably want to keep his child. "I don't even want to marry and make love since it hurts so much," Heather went on.

"It might hurt the first time but when you love someone and do it more often, it doesn't hurt. In fact it feels good." This, coming from a fifteen year old. Heavens to Betsy, Audrey is so outspoken.

We quieted down as dinner was brought to us.

Then Audrey said, "I'm not going to make love to my horse trainer any more if this is what happens, but I sure like to be around him."

"How old did you say he was?" I asked. "You are only fifteen."

"He is nineteen and he teases me a lot and I enjoy the attention."

"Well, look where that attention got you," I told her kiddingly.

EMILY

I was helping Audrey find what talent was available among about one hundred women waiting to give birth. I was good at organizing so Audrey asked me to help. She was used to planning for her horse events. This would take a lot of time trying to catch everyone some time or other and remember who we asked so we didn't keep bothering people.

"Let's start on our wing first since we know them better and see how it works out," she said.

I had my notebook as we shuffled along. Most of us wore slippers with our smocks and our pace was slow and awkward. Some of the girls were outside in the bull pen and some were in the library and some were playing games in the hall.

I exclaimed when I heard someone say she could play the violin which she had brought with her and someone else played the accordion but would have to have it sent. Many said they sang in their church choir. One was a director who would be glad to direct a choir. They would have to decide what kind of music to sing. One girl laughed saying she would do the Charleston dance but couldn't with as big a belly as she had. That was more than I wanted to picture.

Audrey asked, " Who is going to ask permission from Mrs. Haworth?"

I said, "When we have it more planned out, I will ask."

"Where will we hold it?"

She was full of questions.

"We will let Mrs. Haworth decide that. I'm sure it will depend on how large this is going to be," I answered. "Anyway we are getting a good start and it will take several days to get all this down. I'm already exhausted so let's go back to our rooms now."

HEATHER

The girls were meeting again in my room after Emily and Audrey found others who would enter the talent show. They were excited that so many could help out. Another said she would get a few girls to do a skit as she had some training in acting.

I told the girls that people didn't like to watch me sing, they just listened to me, because of my looks.

"I don't believe that," Emily said. "How do you know?"

"Because I've heard them say that. I know I'm large and loud and just plain Jane."

Emily said as she left the room, "I'll be right back. I have an idea."

Audrey and I looked at each other wondering what that could possibly be. Then she came back in with a hand full of all kinds of makeup.

"We just have to enhance your features, Heather," she said. "Let me show you how makeup can help your looks."

"I don't want to wear it as dark as you," I grimaced.

"Don't worry. I know what I'm doing and I will give you a softer look."

Audrey watched while Emily put a light foundation on my face. Then she put a darker foundation on my broad jaws, for contour, she told me. I could already feel a difference. Audrey was fascinated. She didn't wear makeup either but she was so young.

Emily plucked my bushy eyebrows and put some light pencil on to fill them in. I let her put eye shadow on to bring out my green eyes. She then put mascara on my long eye lashes. She outlined the outside of my lips with a pencil to make them look fuller and filled them in with a light pink lipstick. She put some rouge on my cheeks.

As for my hair, Emily took some of my top hair and lowered it over my forehead to the left which helped hide my high forehead.

"Are you ready for a mirror?" she asked me.

"I'm afraid to look. My face feels heavy for some reason."

"Come here and look in the mirror on your dresser and you will be surprised and pleased."

I stood and slowly walked over to the mirror, slowly lifting my head to see in it over the tall dresser. I couldn't get too close to it with my big stomach but I couldn't help but beam. "Oh, my word!" I exclaimed. "I can't believe I can look like that. It's so natural, really. Even my dull brown hair looks brighter."

The end result was a soft look all over and now my glasses didn't over power me. They just seemed to fit in.

"Will the makeup make my acne worse?" I asked.

"You don't have to wear it everyday, just when you want to dress up or go out, you know. But you can enhance your features with mascara and lipstick daily if you want."

"So," Audrey said smiling, "everyone will be happy to watch you sing at the event."

I sang "do re me fa so la ti do" in perfect pitch. I could hardly wait to go to dinner so everyone could see me. They probably wouldn't know me.

"I can't make myself up like this everyday but I will buy some makeup and use it for special occasions. You will have to show me how, Emily. I wasn't looking."

"Be glad to Heather."

"We better not wait too long for this talent show as many who signed up will have had their babies and gone home."

CORA

I received a disturbing letter from some past customers that I wanted to share with some of my staff. I made arrangements with Mrs. Dysart, Mrs. Lowe and Mrs. McEwen to have lunch with me in my dining room downstairs. I liked to meet with them there periodically so they could relax and we could catch up with news of our families and also any problems they were having at the hospital.

Cecil, the cook, brought us a casserole to enjoy while we visited.

I started by asking," Remember that couple a few years ago from Pawnee, Oklahoma who adopted a boy from us? The parents worked with Buffalo Bill in Wild West shows."

"Yes, I remember them," Mrs. Dysart said. "They had lost a boy at six weeks of age so they chose to adopt a boy."

"According to this letter, little Billy also died. He and his friend had been playing cowboy as they usually did on their five hundred acres and Billy tied a rope to a tower a little higher than he was tall and the other end to his neck. He must have fallen and his neck was broken. He was just eight years old."

"Oh, my," Mrs. Lowe said. "I'm so sorry to hear that."

"His mother went on to say how much they loved him. He had everything: a pet alligator, bison, horses, dogs, a black bear, chickens and coyotes. He just loved that place. He got to meet governors, well-known artists and Wild West show stars. He was well-known to his father's show business friends who referred to him as Pawnee Bill, Jr, or the Lieutenant."

Mrs. McEwen said she remembered their home was referred to as a "Mansion."

"What a shame," I said, "that he could have had so many opportunities in life and went to be with our Lord so early. EP is going to feel so disheartened over this. He is so sensitive."

I reached for the latest poem he'd written for his book, Sunshine and Roses," called, "Dead" and I read it to the girls.

Listless the eye, and idle tongues,
Silent the hands that ever moved,
Placid the countenance, now stilled
The palpitating heart that loved.

Dead, do you say? It cannot be
She who was e'er the morning ray,
Dissipating my gloom-set night,
Now is the pulseless, moldering clay!

Dead? Then lift her up carefully,
Bear her gently o'er the sod,
Lower her slowly, silently
Down 'neath the heartless, cruel clod.

Dead! - To meet eternity, -
Yes! - Then a final, long embrace!
And place in my arms my darling child!

That created a long silence.

"What timing that was, Mrs. Haworth. I wonder if it would be appropriate to send it to Billy's parents?" Mrs. Dysart asked.

I was pensive. "Hmmmmm. I will have to ponder this. I need to respond in some way. It's too late to send flowers as the funeral has already happened. In fact, all the third-grade students walked from the ranch to the cemetery."

"I just don't like to hear such bad news of our babies," I sighed.

CORA

I took food home from the kitchen to feed the family that evening and also took a long letter from a Mr. Halbert from the Council of Social Agencies in Kansas City. I sat with EP on the davenport in our large bedroom upstairs to discuss another episode of business problems.

Mr. Halbert was writing to the director of the State Children's Bureau Board of Control in St. Paul, Minnesota, Mr. Charles Hall. He'd written that

> *About four years ago we got a law passed providing that maternity hospitals must have a license from the State Board of Charities and Corrections. Our state board has been trying to build up the standards of these commercial maternity hospitals and has really done quite a good deal to establish good medical care for the girls and their babies and has reduced the evil of exploitation and extortion.*
>
> *The children's bureaus of various surrounding states have written letters to the State Board of Charities and Corrections and also*

to our local social agencies here in Kansas City objecting to the fact that these commercial maternity hospitals run advertisements in their respective states and especially to the fact that they advertise babies for adoption.

..........................Recently the Board has made a new ruling which forbids these hospitals from running any advertisements about babies for adoption at all.

In Missouri all adoptions have to be legally consummated by the Juvenile Court...........................and the custom has been for people of other states to come to Kansas City and then take their babies home to their respective states.

The practice has resulted in making some bad placements............................The judge of the Juvenile Court expects to establish a rule that any prospective foster parents who want to adopt children in Kansas City must first get approval of the children's bureau of their home state before they will be given any child from here.

Yours sincerely,
L.A. Halbert, Executive Director
Council of Social Agencies,
Kansas City, Missouri

EP finished reading the lengthy letter before replying, "It seems like there are always going to be new regulations. At least he is trying to get all of the states children's bureaus to agree. I don't know what this has to do with the hospitals advertising that they have babies for adoption though. We stopped using the newspaper and rely on our pamphlets now that we send to 25,000 doctors around the country. They could be referring to the other commercial hospitals." EP came to The Willows the following day and dictated a letter to Mrs. McEwen to reply to Mr. Hall.

Dear Mr. Hall,

Our Judge Porterfield of Kansas City reports to us that you have agreed to co-operate with him and any local institution here in the investigation of applicants for the adoption of babies, when made by the people living in your state....................................

..........................Now, I do not know your methods sufficiently to know what your procedure will be but judge it will include a personal visit to the applicants in their home by one of your visiting inspectors. We wish you to know that our adoptions are of babies from birth unto a few months old, they rarely remain in our care for longer than six months or a year........................We do not require the usual three months trial placement necessary for older children. Our approval of homes should be final when the child is taken. That makes our work a little more exacting and means a higher grade of references......................................

In placing children of the exceptional class that we get, there is one important thing that I would like emphasized and this is the matter of confidential handling of the adoption. Frequently patrons do not desire it be known that the child comes from The Willows, which may brand it as born out of wedlock.....................................

Just one more point I wish to emphasize, and that is the fact that we will much appreciate the promptness with which your department can pass on applicants. Many of our patrons desire the new, fresh, fine looking baby from 10 days to 30 days after birth....................

Thanking you for any assistance you may render us and assuring you of our co-operation with you,

I am Fraternally yours,
E.P. Haworth,
Supt. The Willows

A week later, we couldn't get over what came back from Minnesota this time.

> *My dear Mr. Haworth - Mrs. Hall went on via two large paragraphs and then suggested one of The Willows babies may be one of incest relations or who is the issue of insane or feeble-minded parents.*
>
> *..............................No woman pregnant with child shall be admitted or received in any licensed maternity hospital or other institution unless prior to her admissions therein, she agrees to feed such child from her own breasts during the period she may be confined in such hospital or institution.*
>
> *The State Board of Control has also stated that every such child shall be nursed by its mother for three months.*
>
> *.........................The practice of parents wanting fresh babies is abhorrent to the standards and principles upon which Minnesota deals with these cases.*
>
> *.................I am sending a copy of this letter to Mr. L. A. Halbert, Executive Director, Council of Social Agencies and also to Judge Porterfield, Judge of the Juvenile Court of Kansas City,*
>
> *Very truly yours,*
> *Charles F. Hall, Director*

Several more paragraphs ensued and then EP continued:

> *Like your own laws ours makes the adoption final so far as I can understand it other than the question of defectives. It safeguards your citizens as well as other citizens against the child that develops and proves imbecilic, or otherwise seriously defective within the period of five years after adoption. This law is probably better than your own law in that an infant might not in all cases show imbecility until it was some months or perhaps two or three years old. This law means that the child can be returned to its mother (since we take no*

responsibility for deformed or defective children). In cases of incest, as suggested by you, will say that we assume no responsibility for the adoption of these children where they can be discovered and the fact that the mothers are with us usually for some weeks or months generally makes these cases discoverable when not explained. The facts usually leak out anyway........................... Our effort has always been that of co-operation with any public official or social agency with which we have had location to deal.

Relative to the mothers nursing the babies, will say that this is our general practice at The Willows, only with the higher-grade patients such as we have, we cannot insist on their remaining for an indefinite or definite extra period with us............................ Another danger in requiring mothers to stay for a prolonged period and nurse their babies is that you force the development of mother love and maternal instincts. Some would infer that this should be done and every effort made to force the mother to keep her child. Perhaps this is justified in many cases but is not true with the larger part for patients. For as you can understand, Mr. Hall, to force a mother of high standing, with education and exceptional opportunities for service in life, to become attached to her child in such a way that she can never go back into perform straight-out life again is neither advantageous to her nor to society in the long run.

Our experience has been that the earlier we can get these babies placed in homes the better for the babies, providing of course that they are kept long enough that the mother and the family can make a final decision as to whether they will give the child up for adoption. Then the sooner the mother is separated from it so she will not develop the mother love for it and grieve over it all her life or try afterwards to interfere with the foster parents' control over it, the better it is for all interested parties.

We have found that if such a place as ours does not exist, many of these higher-grade patients either are forced into the hands of the abortionists out of self-respect, or at the end of their pregnancy term will have to go to some irresponsible cheap rooming house, or to some old granny or outlaw midwife, to be cared for through confinement with the attendant demoralization and serious death rate of both children and mothers.

Mrs. Hall, I believe you will find out of the "interesting Willows statistics" which, if you will take time to look through carefully, I believe will give you better understanding of our work than I can give you by letter.

Thanking you sincerely for your letter and the spirit of co-operation you have indicated your willingness to exercise in our behalf, and trusting we shall soon have details ironed out until there is complete understanding of how to proceed, I am,

Fraternally yours,
E.P. Haworth, Supt.

From L. A. Halbert, Executive Director -

Dear Mrs. Hall,

I have talked the matter over with Judge Porterfield and we are in sympathy with your idea of trying to maintain a high standard of care for the children and of justice to the foster parents.......................

The judge plans to make the requests through his child placing agent, Miss Mary Hudson, instead of having Mr. Haworth ask you for the information....................

Mrs. Haworth will want to have the cases of the girls handled in a confidential manner so as not to embarrass the girls and Miss Hudson will facilitate this desire as much as is consistent with a proper study of the circumstances of the child and mother..............

It will be impossible for us to realize your standards completely, but what we are doing and proposing to do is a great gain over what we have had, and we earnestly request your patience and indulgence so that we may progress without getting into a court fight with these maternity hospitals.......................

Yours sincerely,
L.A. Halbert

HEATHER

I heard my name called over the intercom to go to Mrs. Haworth's office. I had no idea why and wondered what I had done now. Why did I always feel that I had done something wrong? Maybe because I was always getting into trouble at home, not purposely, but I never could do anything right according to my father.

Mrs. Haworth had me sit down which I clumsily did, while she closed the door. She looked very somber.

"Heather," she solemnly said.

"Your mother called. You have probably heard on the news that there has been a stock market crash?"

"No, I have been so busy with our talent show, I haven't heard any news on the radio."

"Your father lost everything and I have very bad news for you. He committed suicide, dear. I hate to be the one to tell you but your mother wanted me to before you call her."

I was sobbing uncontrollably by now. Mrs. Haworth gave me some tissue and came around from her side of the desk to put her arms around me. She smelled so good with her nice perfume.

She said she thought of the girls as her girls and thought we were unfortunate enough in this world without having more problems.

"You cry all you like," she said. "I will go get you some water. Just stay here a while dear."

She went out of the room to give me some privacy. She brought me some cold water and left it on the desk for me.

When she came back about thirty minutes later, I was talking to Mother on the phone in the hall that was used by all of the patients. I was crying some more and saying, "No, no, please no. I am singing in the talent show here Mother. I have found friends here. I have only about six weeks left. Please let me stay here."

I hung up and went to my room where I sobbed with such heart break into my pillow.

Emily heard me and asked what was wrong. I told her between sobs and Emily put her arm around me and wept with me. Then Emily wondered out loud if her parents had lost any of their money also. She said she would worry about that later. "You need me now," she said.

My roommate, Audrey, entered and also wondered what was causing me to be so sad. When she heard, she felt compassion for me too and when I announced I had to move to the charity hospital, Audrey said, "No, you can't do that when we are almost ready to have the show. You are the reason for this."

"I don't want to leave either. I begged my mother but she said I had to as quickly as possible. Mrs. Haworth offered me a cottage room at less expense but Mother said she can't even afford that. I'm just miserable," and I started sobbing again.

CORA

I knew Heather's mother was sending Heather to the state hospital for charity patients. She told me she was desperate. She didn't know what she was going to do. She had to find a family member to live with who wasn't crushed in the crash. I suggested Heather be able to stay in the cottage that was less expensive but Heather's mother said no. She had to have complete charity.

I talked to Mrs. Dysart, Mrs. McKwen and Mrs. Lowe about this and they all felt empathy for Heather.

"Why can't we have a cab bring her back for the talent show, at least?" Mrs. McKwen contributed. "After all, it's because of her voice that they are having this."

"I hope she agrees to that," I said. "I know some Methodists who are trying to get a music school started. I'm going to see if someone can be here that night. They might agree to give her a scholarship in the near future."

"What a grand idea," Mrs. Lowe replied. "I can hardly wait."

I stood up to dismiss them and said I would talk to Heather about the idea as soon as she was ready to move to the Florence Crittenton home.

EMILY

I called my parents to find out if they lost everything in the crash. Heather's dad's suicide caused me to feel frightened to call my folks but surely Mother would have called Mrs. Haworth if he had done anything that stupid.

My mother was concerned but as she explained, my father didn't trust the stock market as he wasn't used to using it so he had stashed most of his money away in other places; probably under the mattress, I thought.

The crash of 1929 was almost enough to change my mind about having lots of money and I was going to call Mel anyway but I thought I would wait awhile so he wouldn't think I was calling because my dad had lost money in the crash.

I really had been missing him and the warmth of his arms around me and his tender kisses. Maybe if I didn't call him soon, someone else would grab him.

I would wait until after the talent show. Everyone was getting excited about it. Out of 150 women in The Willows, twenty-five were participating. Audrey found a team who was experienced at decorating. Mrs. Haworth asked Lyle to make a stage at the end of the dining room. It looked like even she was caught up in the anticipation of this event.

We really missed Heather who moved on and wouldn't be singing. Other girls had offered to sing duets, and quartets, and a small choir developed from the girl who would direct. A few of the girls even shopped for matching smocks so they would look like a particular group.

We were aware that some of the girls in the show might just have a child at the last minute. This was inevitable.

The dining room held only sixty-five people at a time so there would be standing room only if they all came. Mrs. Lowe used the intercom to remind everyone the day of the show. It would start at 8:00 p.m. That way we could digest our dinner before having to play our instruments or sing. A few of the parents would also be joining us since they lived close enough to Kansas City to be able to make it a weekend trip.

I went back in my room after the phone call.

CORA

I couldn't believe the rain day after day as I'd complained to myself as I drove to work. It was one of the wettest years in Kansas City. One morning was particularly frightening as there was a four-mile-high cloud in the Northeast according to the radio. I wondered what that meant.

Maybe I could get our engineer, Lyle, to set up the movie projector and show a delightful movie to the girls. We had several reels in the library.

I parked in back and wished we had a garage in which to park my car. I wondered why the hospital windows were so dark. I carefully walked up the dark steps to my office but I saw no lights.

I would have called Mrs. Lowe on the intercom if the power wasn't out. However, I found her in her office.

"Good morning, Mrs. Haworth. Kansas City has had a power outage. The whole city is in the dark but at least it's day time. Did you see that big dark cloud this morning? And tornados are rampant in the Mid-west. Also an earthquake hit on the New Madrid fault which rattled towns in several states."

"Yes, Mrs. Lowe, I saw it. Thanks for all the good news. It must have just happened because we had electricity at home before I left. Is the world coming to an end?"

Later I got a phone call from a new patient who arrived at the Union Station only to be greeted by a lake. I told her to walk to where the yellow cabs were parked and that I was sorry she may have to walk quite a distance. Land sake, I couldn't believe this.

Lyle came in to tell me water was raging down Walnut Street behind the hospital and clogging storm drains. At least we were on a hill. Later it was announced the dam broke on the Blue River.

EP called and said he was watching plows on the street cars push the water off the tracks as they traveled by the house.

The day before, I had ordered salt-rising bread from Wolferman's grocery to be delivered that day but now I doubted if we'd get it. It would have sure tasted good right then.

EP said he might walk to the nearby coffee shop and watch them grind the beans. He loved to watch the bicycle propped up in front of the mill with a belt connected from the rear wheel to the grinder wheel and see the man pedaling the bike grinding the beans. "What will they think of next? That's real initiative for you," he said.

I was really hungry for salt-rising bread now. I left the radio on all afternoon to listen to the weather. We'd had six inches of rain so far. People were stocking up on coal if they could get it there. Jack Henry's, Rothchilds and Woolf Brothers were advertising sales on over-coats. Sure they were. I would rather shop in snow than rain though.

CORA

Mrs. Lowe, Mrs. Dysart and Mrs. McKwen and I were excited about the talent show the girls wanted to put on. We were discussing the stage Lyle and Ole were building in the dining hall. We also wanted to decorate for them.

"I think this is such a positive thing for the girls. It gives them something else to think about and they have been practicing a lot," I said as I served tea in my Haviland china. "Each time I visit one of the wings I hear someone singing or playing an instrument. EP always put a lot of importance on people to know music in some way. He made sure our children took up some kind of musical instrument."

"Let me read you the first poem in his book, *Sunshine and Roses.* It's called Proem."

Song, song, only song,
Song that cheers the world along;
Simple, light, a word of rhyme,
Blithe as is the gay springtime.

Song, song, just a line,
Lithesome as the bright sunshine;
Fragrance of the springtide rose
And its tint -- just as it grows.

Song, song, light, care-free
As the squirrel in the tree,
Carol of the singing bird,-
Denizen of field and wood.

Song, song, and a smile, --
Help a listless hour beguile,
Though mayhap wayward tear
Smile in memory of a bier.

Song, song -- oh, the grave,
Serious lessons let us cave
For a gloomier day than this
Rainbow-tinted day of bliss!

Song, song -- ah, with me
Sing a song full joyfully!
Where the sun shines brightest, grows,
Thriving most, the fragrant rose.

"Lovely," Mrs. Lowe said. "You should find someone who will read it at the show or maybe even EP would read it."

"No, this show is for the patients. So," I continued, "let's discuss the decorating we must do."

"Maybe the girls will want to do that also," Mrs. McKwen piped up. "I heard they had a decorating committee."

Mrs. Lowe suggested we give them an allowance and take them downtown to shop. "They love to shop downtown. Have you seen the cheap wedding rings they wear that they bought at a dime store?"

EMILY

I heard my name called on the intercom and that I had a visitor in the lobby. Surprised, I looked at my bedside clock and it was 7:00 p.m. I wondered if I should clean up a bit, put some makeup on or change my smock. Maybe it was my parents or one of them and I didn't need to dress up for them.

I walked down the corridor to the next hallway and out to the lobby. No one was there. I looked behind the heavy burgundy velvet curtains in the receiving area and was pleasantly surprised to see Mel. I had called him and he was concerned by the way my brain was working as in should or shouldn't I keep the baby?

He had decided to come for the weekend. I greeted him with a hard to reach hug and we sat on the burgundy velvet davenport. In a way I was embarrassed that he had to see me this large with child.

"Why are you here?" I asked. "I just talked to you recently."

"I wasn't satisfied with how our conversation was going," he said as he held my hand. He saw how big my belly was and he gently patted it. It was his child after all. "I think you said you love me. I hope you said you love me."

"I am so confused, Mel. I thought I had to marry a man with the kind of money my parents have in order to be happy. But living here among other well-off women, I see that money isn't the most important thing. And I missed you so much. And then, after the crash and the suicide of one of my friend's father over loss of money, I came to realize love is more important."

Mel hugged me again and said he was so happy.

"Wait though," I said, "I'm not through." I was very adamant about letting him know how I really felt. "I want to finish school and if I keep the baby, I won't be able to. I want to know what you think about my giving the baby up for adoption and then getting married and I can continue school?"

"I don't know how you can think that way!" he said as he sat back and looked me in the eyes. "Our baby is a love baby. Of course we will keep it. I was so afraid I would never see you again and would never see my child grow up."

He sat forward again. "We will make it work," he went on. "I have family who live in our college town and I'm sure one of them, if not more, would be happy to baby sit while you finish school. Besides, tuition won't cost so much married to a faculty member." He smiled.

"That sounds good," I said. "My dad lost some money but not all. He may not even want to send me to school now."

"Ask him, but if he won't I'm sure we can make arrangements. Please say you will marry me and will keep the baby. I don't care what the other faculty members think."

"Oh, Mel, I feel so much freer. I've been worrying for months now. I've been working in the nursery and loving all those babies. It would be so hard to give up mine."

"Ours," he reminded me.

We hugged and sat cozily together for a long time.

HEATHER

I took a cab to The Willows and went in the back door. My coming would be a surprise and my stomach was churning and it wasn't the baby. I saw the dining room set up with a screen in front of the stage upon which someone had painted cartoon figures of pregnant women in positions of singing and playing piano and guitar. It was humorous to be sure and was certain to cause smiles when the audience came in.

The dining tables were removed so more chairs could be added and they were close together in rows. No one should have to stand.

Emily was in Audrey's room. Audrey hadn't been given a roommate since I left a couple of weeks before. I knocked on the door. Audrey said, "Enter." Were they surprised when I entered!

"Oh, my goodness!" Audrey screamed as she worked to get out of her chair. She was finally getting a stomach. She hugged me. "How did you get here and are you gong to sing?"

"Mrs. Haworth sent a cab for me so I can sing," Heather said smiling from ear to ear. "But I came a bit early so Emily can put makeup on me."

"I'll go get it," Emily said as she gradually pulled her large stomach up from the chair. "You'll have to eat dinner with us too."

"Oh, I'm too excited to eat. I can go down with you though."

Emily went after the make-up and brought it back in a container. She put a little more on Heather than she had previously since there would be bright lights on her.

"While she's working," Audrey said, "how do you like the Florence Crittenton home? Did you change your name back to what it was before you came to The Willows?"

"No, I'm keeping Heather but can't use Haworth which sounded so good together. The girls come from poor families so they haven't had the opportunities I've had nor the education, but they are very nice and are just like us, unfortunate women. We still have that in common, and I should deliver shortly."

"What about the food?" Emily asked.

"It's similar but we don't get as much meat as you do here."

"It's time for dinner," Audrey said. "People won't know you, Heather, since even before when Emily made you up the first time, so few saw you."

CORA

EP and I stood in front of the microphone to welcome the guests. We dressed up too out of respect for this important event. I wasn't wearing a white dress but a nice suit. Most of the seats were full. I was looking out for the two Methodist women who were trying to start that music school and who I had invited. EP thought it was grand that several parents were there. To think those folks were going to be grandparents and wouldn't be able to enjoy it. I thought how sad.

One of the patients, who wasn't very far along, volunteered to be emcee. She was very funny as she introduced the talent.

They were saving Heather for the second act and at the end.

Many of the songs were jazz songs popular on the radio. One song was "*Yes, Sir, That's My Baby,*" which brought laughter; others were "*Franklin Street Blues,*" "*I Found a Round About Way to Heaven,*" "*Here Comes Emily Brown,*" which was a Charleston, "*Somebody Stole My Gal,*" "*Flat Tire Blues,*" *and* " *My Man Is Good for Nothin but Love,*" which brought down the house. Another audience pleaser was a satire to the song of "*My Baby Just Cares for Me.*" Some others were "*Baby, Won't You Please Come Home,*" "*Frankie and Johnnie,*" "*Putin' on the Ritz,*" "*Baby Face,*" "*Georgia on My Mind,*" "*Everybody Loves My Baby,*" — anything about babies made the audience laugh. And then there was "*Nobody Knows You When You're Down and Out.*" The violinists played violin sonatas and some church music.

There were laughs when each girl was introduced with the last name of Haworth.

Heather was nervously excited as she waited for her cue. Her mother had sent her a special smock she had made from a couple of old dresses with lace on the edges and it was a pretty green to match her eyes. With her newly made-up face she looked almost beautiful. She had chosen three songs. Now it was her turn.

When she started singing "*Always,*" and she said, "this is for my baby," there was a hush in the room before tears. There had been quite a bit of laughing and clapping and I'm sure Heather wondered why it was so quiet. But her loud soprano voice was so clear she didn't need the microphone and that was such a beautiful song. She then sang "*Ain't Misbehavin',*" for comical relief. She bowed and started walking off the stage when people stood to give her a standing ovation. Heather looked overwhelmed. She walked back and bowed some more and said, "Thank you so much," before walking off the stage.

During intermission punch and cookies were served. I was pleased to see women and I went over to them to ask what they thought of the show so far. They were really impressed but especially with Heather.

"She comes from a very good family," I stated, "and she was going to a girl's school when she had to leave and come here. I am hoping you can find a place for her, if she is interested. You see, her father recently died and she had to move over to the charity hospital to finish her birth and convalescence. We brought her here in a cab to be able to continue helping out the talent show which was really started because the girls realized what a lovely voice Heather had."

They said they would discuss it with the board but felt sure something could be arranged.

" She is almost ready to birth as you can tell so I hope you can find out shortly."

It was time to sit for the second act. More jazz was played. The last song was sung by Heather. She chose "*My Melancholy Baby*" and she got another standing ovation. The audience wanted an encore so she chose "*Someone to Watch Over Me.*" Afterwards it was quiet, like at the end of a prayer. She walked off the stage and then she heard such loud clapping and whistling. She was smiling as she sat down exhausted. She said even her baby seemed to be clapping. It was late when she took a taxi back to her other home.

AUDREY

When I saw what all of those women could do, how they learned to adjust their lives in this setting and kept their humor, I guess I grew up. I didn't have to depend on my parents forever. I didn't need a mammy to do everything for me. I could do things for myself. I could get along with a roommate who was so different from me.

I was used to hearing crying at night and always wondered if the women crying were missing their parents or their lovers. I learned from them that most of the women were in love with the responsible party. Of course Heather wasn't.

I knew I wasn't going back to my trainer as the same person I was when I left. I would not get involved with him again.

I would continue to show horses a couple more years and then perhaps attend school somewhere.

I left my room to go into the hall to find someone to play one of the games with me. I would skip a little if I physically could.

PART TWO

1930 TO 1953

CORA

The times were changing -- another world war was on the horizon and I remembered when we were so busy with patients and babies during the Great War, which brought such an influx of patients. I had recently remodeled some of the hospital for a nice large apartment for Lucille and me. It was too much to expect a nurse to always take care of her at the house and I could take care of her here. EP stayed at the home on Summit Street. He had become a philatelist and was traveling by bus all over the United States gathering first day cover stamps. He kept very busy at it. He still came for dinner on Sundays if he was in town. He also had a secretary, Lillian, who lived on the third floor. She was attractive and rather crippled, one leg shorter than the other.

There were still so many couples who wanted to adopt babies that we had a waiting list. Some had been waiting years as they first tried to get pregnant before trying to adopt. And some got pregnant after they adopted.

Mrs. Lowe, Mrs. McKwen and Mrs. Dysart are still working but Dr. Kepner, who was our on-site doctor passed away in 1931. I found a good doctor from St. Luke's Hospital to deliver our precious babies.

I had a routine and without the rush, was able to be active with the Women's Chamber of Commerce and the Sunshine Club. I stopped wearing those stiff starched uniforms and switched to wearing very smart suits with the jewelry that I loved. I did enjoy shopping at the department stores downtown like Harzfelds and Woolf Brothers.

Lane Bryant had started selling maternity clothes that were two pieces so the girls didn't have to wear those shapeless smocks they hated. Unfortunately the front of the skirt still hiked up as the patient's stomach grew.

Lucille was talented in music and I had her taking lessons in piano and voice at the Kansas City Conservatory of Music. She was slow in school but the teachers let her finish high school even though it was frustrating for them and all of us.

Daughter Ruth was proficient in violin and base viol. She got married right out of high school and Don was going to go into the service.

I was getting more tired going up all the steps from the basement, to the first floor, then to the second floor where the operating rooms and convalescence rooms were and then up to the nursery on the roof.

Maybe with another war coming, I'd get more business. It was still a stigma having a baby out of wedlock but not so much as when we started the hospital. There were many more abortions being performed today since they weren't as dangerous.

This article in the Kansas City Star made our business sound very busy.

YULE GIFTS TO CUDDLE
REQUESTS FOR BABIES TO ADOPT EXCEED THE SUPPLY HERE
As Christmas approaches, Childless Homes Open Their Doors to Take in Permanently the Little Ones.

More babies are sought for permanent adoption in Kansas City this Christmas season than can be supplied by the two principle sources, the Willows and the Fairmount maternity homes.

A baby a day, on an average, has been let for adoption by the Willows in the last six weeks, and the Fairmount home could have met that average if it had had enough babies. As it is, the Fairmount has been providing about twenty babies a month for adoption.

As Christmas approaches, the demand for babies increases from childless parents. Some of them have been waiting for the right sort of baby for months.

"I have a tree, the lights and the gifts," one woman told Mrs. H. S. Lane, superintendent of Fairmount. "All I need now is the baby."

So strong is the demand for squirming, kicking little Christmas gifts that the babies are seldom more than two weeks old before they are adopted at this time of year, Mrs. Lane added. Two-at-a-time adoptions are increasing in popularity, perhaps because of a growing notion that companionship will be an asset in such an upbringing. Only last week a Kansas City woman adopted two 2-week old infants, Mrs. Lane said.

"A child in the home at Christmas seems to complete the picture," Mrs. Lane concluded.

At the Evans Children's Home, not a maternity institution, Mrs. Mary J. Weaver last night reported a lively demand for children for adoption. The home last Christmas season provided twenty-six children from two to five years old for adoption. In the last six weeks eighteen children have been adopted from the Evans home, and a half dozen or more are scheduled for adoption this week.

TRUDY

I entered The Willows in the mid-1940's. I was a typical old maid school teacher and the maternity dresses I wore were just as frumpy as my school clothes. My red hair was my best feature. It was curly and framed my face.

"Mrs. Haworth, I'm so embarrassed. I don't know what my students are thinking of me leaving like I did."

"Didn't you tell them you had to take care of a sick aunt or something like that?"

"No, I didn't think of that."

"You can write the class and explain in a letter, dear. So, let's fill out this paperwork and then Mrs. Lowe will help you to a room. Who is the father of your child?"

"Oh, do I have to answer that? I'm so ashamed. I have a boyfriend but he is overseas with our troops and I was dancing at the USO with a nice young soldier whose girlfriend had just broken off with him. I felt so sorry for him when he told me he was being sent over seas and we got carried away. I don't even remember his name."

Mrs. Haworth was kind. "Oh, that's all right Trudy. Just give me some details on his size, hair and eye color so we can match it up with a family of similar traits. Do you plan to give up the baby?"

"I didn't know I had a choice," I said. "Let me think about that. If my boyfriend comes home early, he may think the baby is his and then I could keep it. Hmmmmmm. How long do I have, Mrs. Haworth, to tell you?"

Cora looked apprehensive. "You can let me know anytime before birth."

"Well, that's a relief," I said. "I have three or four months then. A lot can happen in that time."

"Do you have the support of your parents?" she asked me as she patted her hair.

"Yes, however they don't want my siblings to know. This is a real stigma in our small community."

Mrs. Haworth said, "We don't judge anyone who comes here. We all make mistakes. We are here to help you have a safe pregnancy with our treatments, so when you get married, your husband will not be able to tell you had a baby. There should be no scars and with exercise and not gaining too much weight you should have your body back into shape by the time you leave here ten days after birth."

Mrs. Lowe was introduced to Trudy and took her and her suitcase to a wing of the hospital to find a room with a nice roommate.

"This is Kate and she is about half your age but we are getting filled up. Maybe she could use a parent-type person. I'll let you get acquainted and then I'll show you around the areas you will be using. With all of our latest built-on wings, one can get lost around here."

"Hello Kate. If you are half my age you must be fifteen. You don't have to hide in the corner. Come on over here and show me where I can put my clothes. I don't bite. I'm a school teacher and my students are about your age."

"I'm only fourteen," Kate shyly answered.

"Speak up sugar, I can't hear you,"

"I'm okay. I'd like to help you. I'll move my clothes over to this side of the closet so you can have that side. I'm using only the top drawer of the dresser so you can have the bottom two drawers."

"Well, thank you," I said smiling. "You are right helpful. Would you like to show me around? Have you been here long?"

Kate murmured yes, she could show her around.

"Let's go then. I hope we can meet some other women as we look around," I said.

NANCY

I had a lot on my plate. I had been working, putting myself through college with a major in art. My parents didn't know how I was making money. I didn't want anyone else to know that either. I was fearful my body wouldn't be the same again but this hospital practically guaranteed that with their extravagant offer of spas and massage, no one would be able to tell I gave birth. I felt lucky to have gotten a private room. Since Japan bombed Pearl Harbor, more women were getting into trouble and the rooms were filling fast.

I liked to spend my time in my room drawing cartoons. I wasn't good at close relationships with the other patients. For one thing, I was too ashamed of the work I had been doing to put myself through college.

I was on my way to tell Mrs. Haworth the statistics of the responsible party but not who it was.

The office door was open.

"Come in, Nancy," Mrs. Haworth said. "How may I help you?"

"I want to give you the statistics of my RP which I guess you need in order to find a family to adopt my baby."

As I was leaving Mrs. Lowe went in and told Mrs. Haworth she had to put the new girl in with Kate. She overheard her say, "Maybe Kate will tell her who the RP is."

Mrs. Haworth said, "Thanks for caring enough to think of that. She won't even talk to her father when he comes over. I wonder why her mother doesn't come?"

I walked back to my room and thought there must be someone else keeping a secret besides me.

One of the girls asked me to come out and play cards with them. They needed a fourth for bridge. "What are you doing in there that's more fun?" she asked.

"I'm busy right now. I'll be out later when I get through with this project."

Later I went out to the hall where some of the girls were lounging; someone was painting her nails; another was doing someone's pedicure since a protruding stomach disallowed her to do it herself.

"What is your project?" someone asked me.

"I'll show you when I'm through. It's a fun thing for me and I think you all will like it."

I then asked, "Who will let me use their massage time? I'll pay you."

One of the girls spoke up saying I could use her time. "I don't care what I'll look like after this kid pops out. I don't plan to ever get married anyway."

CORA

I noticed that a class of adoption cases was increasing in numbers and that is where the doctor would write us sometimes, before the patient even entered the sanitarium, that he had a home for the child. And we encouraged him in such cases to take the matter up directly with the mother or her people themselves and eliminate us from all connection with the adoption.

If the mother wished to keep her child in reach of her where she could have it later on and was sure she could manage this without eventually exposing her misfortune to the public with the reflection on herself and her child, it was likely to be desirable. But if the child was placed with acquaintances of hers, or with friends of theirs, with the expectation that it was permanent, the hazards were so great that The Willows' management asked to be left entirely out of the matter other than providing seclusion and hospital services.

After all those years in adoption work we had become wise to many unexpected possibilities. We early on learned that we should not place a baby born of a Kansas City mother with people living in Kansas City, even as large a city as it was. It would be even worse in a smaller community. But since the state took over, we had no more say who the adoptive parents were. I think I was much more careful.

If a man wanted to get hold of his child, the law gave him that right only through marriage. When he was not married to the girl, he certainly had no moral right to the child conceived and born out of wedlock.

Never was a baby placed with patrons of The Willows who came and called for some particular child, when there was the least shadow of possibility of the case being traced back to a friend of the child's mother.

Whatever criticism might be offered the individual who has succumbed to sex temptations, there could be no question that the greatest individual sufferer was the unwelcome child. Though condemning the guilty parents, one must feel the need of sympathy and assistance for that mite of humanity who must be the innocent victim of its origin.

TRUDY AND KATE

Mother forwarded letters to me from my boyfriend, Frank, who was overseas. That way he still thought I was at home. I couldn't sleep nights wondering what would happen to my baby; should I have told Frank I was pregnant with his child so if he got back before the baby was born, he wouldn't be surprised? I just couldn't do that yet. I was so scared. I wouldn't know until the last minute and I could always put it up for adoption and go home and wait for Frank.

Nancy came over and I wondered what she wanted. We never saw her unless she wanted something. "Hi Nancy, come on in."

"Hi Trudy. How are you feeling? Have you heard from your boy friend lately?"

"No, not for a while," I said. "Why?"

"I know he's over seas. Are you going to be using your massage time this week?"

"Yes, Trudy. I love the massages and spa baths they give us. Why?"

"I like them too and am willing to pay for any extras someone might want to give up. I'll look for Kate. She might be willing."

Nancy found Kate in the library where she could hide from all the activity. She read a lot in there rather than taking books back to her room.

"Hi Kate. What are you reading?"

" I brought some books from home and like to read in here where there's more privacy. Why do you ask?"

"Just curious what a young girl likes to read these days."

"This is a Nancy Drew mystery. I love her books. I have them all so far. Sometimes I read them over again."

"Well, I really want to know if I can pay you for your spa and massage time."

Kate looked surprised. She said shyly, "Well, I don't know. We all need to have them so our scars and birth marks won't show when we get married someday. Let me think about it, maybe occasionally."

"Okay," Nancy said as she tossed her long blonde hair over her shoulder. "Let me know if you change your mind. I'll go ask around."

KATE

I felt so lonely. I was the youngest woman in here and I was so ashamed of who the father was. I wasn't sure if Mrs. Haworth would have let me in if she knew. I just couldn't tell anyone yet. I didn't know what to do. Should I have said something to someone? But to whom? Mother would never have believed it. I didn't want to go home but I didn't know where else I could go. I wasn't old enough to get a job. I liked my roommate. She was motherly. I was also missing out on school. How was I going to make it up and explain to my friends how I got behind?

I told Mrs. Haworth I didn't see the man who got me pregnant. He forced himself on me in the dark, which was true. I couldn't give her any information for the adoptive parents. My daddy kept telling my family it must have been one of my brother's. How dare he suggest that! My mother called me a tramp. I didn't think I was wanted at home. Mother didn't even kiss me goodbye.

Daddy was well-known in our small town. He couldn't get me out of there fast enough. He said I went to take care of a sick aunt, as if I was old enough to care for an adult who was sick. I was also very small. I loved school and I missed that and my friends. I wondered what they would think when I went back. I couldn't go back. I had to go somewhere else. But where? I had relatives in lots of midwestern towns. Would any of them want to take me in?

I missed my kitty and I'm sure she missed me. Wherever I went, I wanted to be able to take her with me.

Oh, I wished I were dead. I still felt like a little girl and I'd been told that because I wore braids. I couldn't believe I was going to have a baby. I was still a baby.

I asked Mrs. Haworth who would be adopting my baby. She said she didn't know but my child would get a good home. I asked her if it would be someone who lived in a town near us, and she said when she had control over who the adoptees parents were, she made certain they were from far away from where the mother lived, but now that the county had taken over the adoptions, she had no control. That worried me a lot. Daddy wanted some friends of his to adopt my baby. That would have been awkward.

I went out to the hall to see if anything was happening?

"Did I just see a cat out here?" I asked one of the girls.

"Yes, that's Stubby. See, she doesn't have much of a tail. She is the house mouser but during the day she comes up from the kitchen downstairs and hangs around."

I was so excited. Something to play with. "I'd like to go find her. Will she play with me?" I asked.

"You can try. She's not real playful because most of the girls just ignore her."

I found her in one of the rooms and picked her up. She was gentle and not very large. Her gray fur looked silver in the light. "What a pretty kitty," I told her as I petted her. "Come into my room if you want company. No one is in here."

I took her back to my room and she shyly inspected it, occasionally wagging her stub of a tail. She seemed to like the closet but then came out again. She didn't want to be held and she left and went back downstairs.

CORA

I was having problems with one of the nurses. She was a pill for sure but I didn't know why? She went through our training school and didn't become a pill until afterwards. She went home for quite a while before she returned to work with us. I made a mental note to ask Mrs. Dysart to try to find out.

It was nice to be busy again but it was too bad it had to be a world war that brought on the patients. I had heard that the other homes made the patients feel guilty. I didn't believe in that. They were just unfortunate they got into that mess. I thought of my granddaughter, Beverly, who was a teenager. I had told her not to let a boy kiss her. She said, "I don't grandmother. I kiss them." She is such a sweetie but I worried about her. Her dad was so strict with her because his sister had a baby out of wed lock. She kept her baby and her dad was a Methodist minister. I was surprised they allowed her to do that. She and the child even lived at home with them. I don't think Bevy knew that because she wrote me about the strictness of her parents. We had a young girl at the hospital who reminded me of Bevy.

"Come in Mrs. Lowe. What can I help you with?"

"Guess what? Stubby is laying outside Mary Ann's room. So, Mary Ann must be ready to deliver soon. I wonder if she knows that?"

"Stubby is never wrong. Did Mary Ann see the cat?"

"Not yet. Her door is closed. I'll check on her though to see how she is. She is due to give birth soon."

"Ok. Let me know, will you?"

"Sure."

We didn't know how that cat knew when someone was going into labor. She just knew. But why would she even bother to lie outside the door for hours sometimes? Otherwise she was a good mouser.

NANCY

My stomach was getting pretty large fast it seemed. I was so stressed about it. My job to get me through college just wouldn't allow for any scars to show and I had to keep my figure. The other girls weren't letting me buy their massage time like I thought they would. Money usually bought anything.

The girls thought I was too withdrawn so I decided to draw them some cartoons and that might help them like me and maybe that would buy me some massage time.

I got down to business and the time went so quickly as I had so much fun drawing, especially cartoons.

I went out to the hallway with some of my drawings to see who was there. Four were playing Bridge and a Canasta table was set up. They seemed very engrossed in their thinking, especially the Bridge players. Maybe I shouldn't have butt in. But I did.

"Hey girls," I called. "I'd like to show you some funny pictures I made if you can spare a minute."

I sat down near them and brought them up, one by one.

"Oh, my gosh," one said. "This stomach looks just like a basketball. I suppose mine will look like that someday."

"Oh, I like the one where you drew hearts on the stomach. That's really sweet."

"I see she can't get behind the steering wheel of a car, she's so big."

"Another shows two women trying to meet but their stomachs get in the way."

"And that one shows the baby inside kicking. That's mine for sure. You have quite a gift, Nancy."

"Yes, you should show these to Mrs. Haworth. I bet she would laugh."

"Thanks girls. I enjoy doing these. Maybe I could hang them up in this hall for now. Do you think anyone would mind?" I asked.

"Heck no. I'll get some tape for you. I can't wait for the floor nurse to see these."

I went back to my room, not wanting to take advantage of them at that moment to buy massage time.

TRUDY

I decided to call home. My parents knew about my predicament since I lived at home. They knew I was old enough to know better but they also thought it was Frank's baby.

"Hi Mom, it's me. How are you and Pop?"

"We're doing fine. We think of you a lot. We are forwarding Franks's letters to you but have you told him about the baby?"

"I don't want to worry him about it while he's overseas," I answered deciding that should take care of that.

"But, Trudy, dear, it might give him joy and a reason to live and fight to get this war over with soon."

"I'll think about it. Do any of my friends and relatives living in that town know about me?"

"No, dear, we haven't told a soul. They think you are on a sabbatical."

"So, wouldn't they be surprised if I came home with a baby?" My mother hadn't thought that apparently.

"My roommate here is only fourteen and she is so frightened. I don't know if it's because she's so young and afraid or what? She won't talk. Mrs. Haworth hopes she will confide in me with who the baby's father is. She won't even see her own father when he comes to visit. She is strange."

"You are a motherly type, school teacher and all, so maybe she will look up to you and tell you sometime. Just be patient."

"Thanks, Mom. I'll call you again soon. Say hi to Pop."

I was supposed to be a grownup and more sure of myself but I was too scared of when the baby came if I'd want to keep it and tell Frank it was his. What if it didn't look like either of us? I told this to Mrs. Haworth and she said that adopted children take on the ways of their new parents like walking and talking like them, their facial expressions, and so forth. So not to worry.

Kate came back from the library.

"Trudy, do your mom and dad care about you having a baby out of wedlock?"

"Well, yes, they care. They sent me here early so my younger siblings wouldn't know. They tell everyone I'm on sabbatical. Why?"

"My mother thinks I'm a tramp and she won't have anything to do with me. I don't know what I'll do when I leave here. I can't go home."

"What does your father think?" I asked.

"I don't want to talk about him."

"He comes to see you Kate. He must think a lot about you. Your mother doesn't come, I noticed."

"Daddy is all for the baby and wants some friends of his to adopt it. That would be absolutely horrible. I don't want to see that child growing up in my town."

"Tell Mrs. Haworth that you don't want it to be adopted by friends of his. I'm sure she will understand."

Kate left crying and I'm not sure where she went. I wished I could've helped her.

CORA

I called EP to inform him of the letter I got from the fire department with new regulations. We had to plaster the boiler room and make it fireproof. Maintenance was getting so expensive since the building was getting so old.

And it was so hot in there. I had fans going everywhere for the patients and one in my office and in my apartment and of course for Lucille. And I carried a hand fan. My bracelets were always jingling because I was always fanning myself.

I had to drive over to my daughter-in-law Peggy's one night and had trouble seeing with car lights in my face. I later called the eye doctor and he said I probably had cataracts. I made an appointment to see about that.

Mrs. Dysart told me she talked to the nurse who didn't seem happy and took it out on everyone else. The nurse wouldn't tell her anything or didn't know of anything to tell.

I was also worried about our son, Don, who was in the army. He looked so handsome in his uniform. He would be coming home soon after his two-year tour of duty. I hoped he would help me here in the office.

EP said I was a worry wart and I suppose I was. But he no longer had the responsibility for the hospital.

We rarely spoke any more. I was sad about that because he was always so attentive. I missed that. It's nice, though, that I get some affection from my staff and the girls. It's usually a joy to visit them and see how well they are doing.

And I kept in touch regularly with my sisters and a brother.

NANCY

I'd been invited to a confab with some others meeting in the bull pen outside. It was a beautiful day and I saw there were a bunch of girls out there. They looked serious. I thought it must be cooler out there since there was a breeze.

"What's going on?" I asked.

"We are just wondering about our lives after this like: will we tell our husbands when we marry? After all, we are trying to get out of here without scars they tell us."

Everyone had a different question.

"Will we worry about what happens to our child as he grows up?"

"I was adopted myself and I had good parents. I'm not worried about my baby getting good parents."

"Will we feel guilty all our lives?"

"There are so many questions that are unanswered. We don't know who to ask."

"What is labor like? Will we have to go through that all alone? We never hear from anyone after they have their baby. I hear we have to be here ten days. Will we be asked to nurse our baby?"

"Will we even be allowed to nurse?"

"I don't know if I want to nurse my baby."

"I don't even want to see my baby," Kate said.

"Don't want to see your baby you've been carrying around all these months? I can't believe it."

Kate looked down and said, "It's not a love baby. And I don't want to love it."

"Hold on there everyone," I said as I dropped down on a chair nearby. "Maybe we should ask Mrs. Haworth?"

"Mrs. Dysart is in charge of the nurses. Maybe she would know more."

"What about the library? Surely we can find some books there or ask for them."

"What would we ask for?"

The questions wouldn't stop and I finally went back inside but tried to figure out how we could find some answers.

CORA

I had so much happening. I called my daughter-in-law Peggy for her help.

"Good day Peg. Can you come over? I'm going to need some help and need to talk to you here and show you some things."

"Good, I'll see you soon."

Peggy and I went down the hall into my office so as not to disturb Lucille. I closed the door which was unusual for me and Peg could tell something was wrong.

"Are you feeling all right?" Peg asked me.

"Yes and no. Lucille needs gall bladder surgery and I need cataract surgery. This has hit me like a bomb shell all of a sudden. I am hoping you can stay here a few days while I go through this and after Lucille's surgery and she recuperates, I will need transportation to the doctor for my cataracts. Also while the optometrist checked my eyes for that he found out I have glaucoma."

"I am so sorry to hear that," Peg said. "Of course I will help. Daughter Carol will come to work with me. She can be with Lucille and help her too. Since she was adopted from here, it will be good for her. What is the prognosis for Lucille?"

"The doctors aren't worried. They tell me it's just normal procedure. She is so hard to take care of now because of her handicap so it will be harder afterwards until she gets her strength back. She is getting heavier and I put a girdle and hose on her every day and a pretty dress. She is able to help somewhat. She may just have to wear smocks for a while after surgery. She is in a wheel chair most of the time. She just can't do crutches much any longer."

"Let me know what you want me to do on the business part and we can do that over several days."

"Peg, you know Mrs. Dysart, Mrs. McKwen and Mrs. Lowe could run this hospital since they have been here for so long. I just need you to be here for them and I'll give you my daily schedule."

KATE

My name was being called over the intercom. I wondered what Mrs. Haworth wanted? I went to the office to see and found my father waiting for me there. I turned to go back to my room.

"Oh, no you don't," someone said as my arm was grabbed. I looked up and saw Mrs. Lowe.

"Your father has been here to see you a number of times and you won't come out. Now that I've got you, I will take you to him."

"No, Mrs. Lowe. I hate him. Don't make me talk to him," I cried.

"You can't hate your father," she said as she dragged me along.

"Hello Kate," my father said as Mrs. Lowe dropped me off at the reception area.

"Hi, dad. I've told you I don't want to see you. Why do you keep coming?" I asked as I started biting my nails.

"I want to apologize to you, Kate. I was drunk that night and thought you were your mom, when I crawled into bed with you. I'm so sorry and I've quit drinking. I don't even remember what happened. I was in a black out."

"Well, I remember," I said emphatically. "And I don't like to think about it."

"Of course you don't."

I heard the grandfather clock in the foyer strike three. How long was he planning to stay?

"Did you ever tell Mom? She thinks I'm a tramp and won't talk to me."

"No, I can't tell her that I'm the father."

"She should understand since you've been drunk so often."

"Well, I have friends in town who would like to adopt your child."

"I don't want anyone I know to adopt it. I don't want to be reminded of it," I wailed. I couldn't believe this. Why would he want to see it? "I'll tell Mrs. Haworth to be sure no one near my town adopts it."

"Mrs. Haworth doesn't have anything to do with that. It's done through the Jackson County Juvenile Court," he told me.

I was trying to hold in my tears. I wished my mother would come visit. She would never forgive me. And if she knew it was dad's child, she wouldn't forgive him either. Maybe I should have told her. I never wanted to see him again.

"Just keep out of this, Dad. I'm going back to my room. Don't bother to come here again. I don't want to see you or be reminded of how I got pregnant. I don't even want to come home again," I said as I left and ran back to my room. At least I knew he didn't do it on purpose. But I still couldn't stand to think of it.

CORA

Lucille was taken to the hospital yesterday for preparation. She told me that an angel had visited her during the previous night and asked her if she was ready to go home with her. She said she told the angel yes. I didn't know what to think of this. The surgery was not that serious according to the doctors but Lucille seemed at peace.

I was waiting for her to get out of gall bladder surgery. She was only thirty-two years old. I wasn't worried but of course I felt concern. Peggy was at The Willows, covering for me. Ruthie and her family were on their way driving to Canada.

"Mrs. Haworth," I heard. The doctor was standing there. "Everything went fine. She'll be in recovery for a while. You'll be able to see her soon."

"Oh, thank you doctor. I trusted you to take care of her and thank you so much."

I continued to knit. However, it wasn't much longer before he came back and sat down with me. He looked like he wanted to say something but was having a hard time. He finally told me she died in recovery. "There was no reason for her to die," he said. "She came through the surgery just fine. I'm not sure what happened," he said softly to me.

I felt faint. I just couldn't believe it. She was only thirty-two and it wasn't that serious. I asked to borrow a phone and I called Peggy. She came to the hospital and I had her call EP. Then I was told the highway patrol could look out for Fred and Ruthie and the children if I told them exactly where they were going and from where.

I cried and cried, "Oh, my poor Lucy." She was so sweet and kind. What will I do now? I've taken care of her for so long. It won't be the same without her. I felt devastated.

When EP got there by streetcar, we went in to see our dear child. She looked so peaceful. Then I remembered her dream and I told EP and Peggy. I guess our Lord was ready to take her and now she was walking and running in heaven. What a nice thought, that she was whole finally, after all those years. But we would miss her sweet voice and smile.

That was the longest day of my life. I didn't want to leave her but had to. Peggy took us home in her car. EP looked so soulful as we dropped him off at his Summit Street home.

CORA

Fred and family were still in the states and they turned around to come to Kansas City. It took them a couple of days but they made it back for the funeral. It was just lovely. We had so many people including our staff from The Willows, and people came from the Kansas City Conservatory where Lucille took voice and piano, and our family. Lucille had touched so many people throughout her cheated years. I still wondered why God took her so early. There were so many flowers and the singing and the reverend's sermon were just so meaningful. The funeral home was full.

The family came back to my apartment after we buried Lucille in the cemetery. It was in July and so hot. My dress was clinging to me. Peggy and Ruthie helped me change into a comfortable house dress. We had fans going everywhere.

My cook, Cecil, had made us a wonderful meal of finger foods so we wouldn't have to go downstairs to the formal dining room and could stay in the apartment. The food came up the dumb waiter to my kitchenette outside the back door to my apartment. Cecil made the best cookies.

Ruthie stayed with me a few days and we sorted out Lucille's clothes for charity. She had lovely dresses. Granddaughter Bevy found a ruby ring of Lucille's. I said she could have it since it fit. Bevy was fourteen.

And when everyone had gone, how lonely I felt.

NANCY

Time was going fairly fast. I'd thought it would be so slow since there wasn't anywhere to go and I figured it would be boring in one place for months on end. But there were girls who needed a pedicure, manicure, their hair done and always someone to accommodate. We played games like chess, Who Dunnit, Clue, checkers, card games and Monopoly. I liked going in the evenings to the park on the south side and sitting in the swing and listening to the locusts. The lilac bushes always smelled so good at this time of year. They were so full and I picked some for a vase in my room. At least I had a window and could see the lights of Kansas City downtown since we were on a bluff. I even watched airplanes fly in to the airport across the river from downtown.

I hadn't been eating much and skipped some meals because I didn't want to gain much weight. I prayed my baby would get a good home with Christian parents. I hoped to go back to work but if they found out I had a baby, I was sure I couldn't. I needed just one more year to finish school. I got my work costume out of the drawer and Trudy walked in. Shoot.

"What have you got there, Nancy?" she asked.

"Don't you knock before you come in?" I said and it wasn't in a nice way.

"It looks like a bunny fur," she said as she made herself at home.

I quickly put it back in the drawer and didn't comment.

"What do you want, Trudy?"

"I just wanted to chat with someone. Nothing is happening around here. I feel so bad for Mrs. Haworth losing her daughter so unexpectedly, don't you?"

"Well, of course. But Mrs. Haworth is getting up there in years. She may not be able to take care of her daughter much longer. Maybe God knew it was time. Did you hear about the angel who came to the foot of her bed."

"Yes, that is amazing," Trudy said. "I've never heard of anything like that. By the way, if you want to take my massage time tomorrow, you may. I have other plans."

"Oh, thanks." Nancy smiled. "I'll pay you for it. It means a lot to me."

"Why is it so important to you, Nancy?"

"I just don't want to have any scars showing at all when I leave here, that's all."

"Well, none of us do."

TRUDY

I wondered why Stubby was upstairs. I didn't think any one of us was ready to give birth. She only came when someone was about to go into labor. I saw that she stopped by Vivian's room and wondered.

Now that I was getting closer to labor, I still didn't know what to do about keeping the baby. Frank didn't know when he was coming home. He still had some months before his tour of duty ended. Maybe I should have just told Mrs. Haworth I would give the baby up for adoption. I was so tired of worrying and wondering. With the war going on, Frank could be killed. If it were his baby, I would have wanted to keep it out of love for him. But it wasn't. But if he came home early and found out I was pregnant, he would think it was his and want to keep it of course.

Vivian was in her room and sounded like she was going into labor. I better get the nurse.

Kate came out of her room asking, "What's the commotion?"

"I don't know why Vivian is moaning like that. She's not due for a while but Stubby is outside her door. I'm looking for the nurse."

"I'll go get her. You go help Vivian if you can."

I went into Vivian's room and she was on the bed in a fetal position and groaning.

"What's wrong Vivian?" I asked.

"I don't know for sure. I just got these stomach pains all of a sudden and they are excruciating."

"Kate is getting the nurse. Have you taken anything for them?"

"No, I don't know what to take."

"Maybe you just have gas," I said as I tried to make her comfortable. "Here's the nurse."

Mrs. Dysart, head of nurses, came and said she was going to take her to the delivery room. "She is probably having a miscarriage."

I went back to my room with Kate. We prayed she would not lose her baby however, maybe that was for the best. We prayed for God's will. Kate prayed that she would have a miscarriage.

Then we wondered how Stubby knew. We all thought Stubby knew when water was broken since Manx cats love water. But that must not have been the case. Stubby must have been psychic.

CORA

I called Mrs. Lowe, Mrs. Dysart and Mrs. McEwen in to discuss business and some of the patients.

"Mrs. Lowe, if you go to the dumbwaiter, Cecil sent up some tea and cookies for us."

As we were getting settled I announced, "I'm trying to sell the nursing home. Since the school closed, we don't need it. I've had a few people look at it."

Mrs. Lowe asked, "What would someone else do with it? It is on hospital property."

I reminded her it was in back on the edge of the property and facing Walnut Street. "I suppose it could be a boarding house," I answered as I settled in to my bed where I always sat after I turned on the TV. They sat on the two chairs in my room.

"Well, I hope it's not full of men with our pregnant women coming and going in the back parking area," Mrs. Dysart said.

Mrs. McEwen said, "Maybe it won't be a boarding house. Maybe a large family will buy it and we will hear children's voices for a change."

I said we would hope for the best.

Mrs. Dysart said, “Oh, I found out why that nurse has been such a pill to you, Mrs. Haworth. One of the other nurses told me that when she went home that time for quite a while, she had an abortion. It made her angry each time seeing a patient have a nice baby when she had to have hers aborted because she couldn’t take the time to wait nine months to go back to work.”

“Good grief,” I said. “She is lucky to be alive. Abortions are so dangerous for the mothers. I wonder what we can do to make her feel better? Maybe we will think of something.”

“I want to discuss our young Kate,” I said. “Her father came again and she did speak with him. When I called her on the intercom, I didn’t say who was here for her so she came and saw him and Mrs. Lowe made sure she would stay to hear him out.”

Mrs. Lowe leaned forward and asked, “What do you think he said?”

“I have no idea. I don’t have a way to listen nor do I want to,” I said.

“But, Kate told me her father has friends in her town who want to adopt the baby. I told her in the past, we never let that happen in the same town but now that the juvenile court is in charge of adoptions, there is nothing we can do.”

Mrs. Dysart, my head nurse, said,” there is definitely something bothering her about her father. I haven’t wanted to say this but you don’t think he is the RP do you?”

We all gasped. “Surely not,” I said.

“Well, her mother never comes,” Mrs. McEwen said. “And, Kate keeps saying she can’t go back home.”

I felt just devastated. I thought, that poor child. It was hard to believe. “I’ll have a talk with her soon,” I said.

Mrs. McEwen said, “Congratulations on getting elected president of the Sunshine Club, Mrs. Haworth. You have worked so hard for that club. You deserve it.”

"I really don't have time for it now. We are so busy during this war. And I've had to add a sprinkler system to our hospital as government regulations. I wonder what will be next? I wished we had air conditioning."

Mrs. Dysart said, "We have fans everywhere and by sprinkling water on the tent over the babies beds on the roof, it evaporates and the area is cooled off. It's better for them than having them inside. It's so much hotter upstairs."

I told them, "I helped with a hard delivery last night. It just wore me out. Joelle had a very big baby and a very hard time pushing it out. I held her hand and wiped her brow. She is such a small person and had a ten pound baby boy. And speaking of babies, EP's secretary is pregnant. I suppose I should offer her free delivery."

I wondered how she met someone? She has only Sundays off. Being handicapped, where does she go and what does she do? Where would she find someone?

"I also want to know if you have any idea why Nancy wants so many massages? It doesn't make sense to me. Mrs. Lowe told me she is paying the girls to give up their time for her."

"She is also worried about her breasts getting larger and getting stretch marks." Mrs. Lowe said. "She has a beautiful figure but she is only going to college. Most of the patients are concerned about their bodies after birth but Nancy is obsessed with hers."

"I wish the girls wouldn't sell their time. They may regret it later," I added.

NANCY

I wondered if Trudy had figured out why I had a piece of clothing that looked like bunny fur. I hoped not. I didn't think I would ever fit back into that costume.

Mrs. Haworth didn't look good. She acted like she was wearing down and she didn't come by so often to see "her girls."

I was sure the loss of her daughter had taken a tole on her. Did she not think we would feel the loss of our babies? But hers had lived thirty-two years so she had longer to be with her and would miss her more I guessed.

My RP gave me the money to pay for this hospitalization, thank goodness. Since he was married, he didn't want anyone to know so he gave me cash -- lots of it. I wasn't supposed to get serious with any customers. I worried I'd have to get a job at a different location when I returned and that I'd need a larger costume. Just one more year then I could teach art. My goal was so near. I prayed nothing more would get in the way of it.

CORA

I was having so much trouble with my feet. I went to a doctor regularly for treatment. It hurt to walk and my blood pressure was so high. The doctor told me to drink coffee upon arising for my headaches. I was afraid of having a stroke. I was in my early seventies so was not surprised, but I still had so much to take care of. I finally sold the nursing home for $15,000. Then I could pay one of the doctors the $650 I owed him. Selling the home was a relief, money-wise, since I was not now responsible for all of the nurses living there. Those who weren't married and living elsewhere would have to find an apartment or house somewhere and commute to work. That would also help not having to have meals for them.

I was so happy Ruthie and Fred and children were coming for a visit. We planned to have dinner at the Town House with my sister, Virginia, who was head of housekeeping there. They were such a sweet family and I so enjoyed having them here.

But my headaches were so bad.

I called Kate to come in to my office. I had to find out about her problem. I couldn't let it go and get worse.

"Come in Kate," I said nicely as she came to the door after hearing her name called on the intercom. "Please take a seat. May I get you some water?"

"No, thank you. Did I do something wrong?"

"No, dear, why would you think that?"

"When my mom or dad called me in it was because I did something wrong."

I felt bad because she may have done something wrong but it wouldn't have been her fault, I didn't think.

"Kate, we at The Willows want to help our girls. That is our goal and desire and always has been. We are concerned about you because you won't tell us who the responsible party is for your pregnancy and you won't see your father when he comes. Also your mother never comes. By putting two and two together, we are wondering if your father is the RP."

Kate started crying and I put my arms around her. "Don't be ashamed, Kate. These things happen. We want to know how to help you so please be candid with me so that I can."

"Oh, Mrs. Haworth," she sobbed, "I feel awful. But when he came and finally talked to me, thanks to Mrs. Lowe who insisted that I listen, he apologized and said he was drunk and thought he was in bed with my mom but he won't tell her so she thinks I'm a tramp and calls me that. She didn't even kiss me goodbye."

Oh dear, I wished Mrs. Lowe and Mrs. Dysart were in here with me.

"Kate, we never wanted to place a baby that was conceived that way. And I don't think we have. However, we have nothing to do with that since the county now places our babies."

"Oh, no, Mrs. Haworth," she sobbed. "My dad has neighbors who want to adopt my baby. I don't want to live there and see it grow up."

"No, that wouldn't be prudent," I said. "I'll talk to the social worker and see what I can do about that. Surely they can take this into consideration. Don't you worry."

"What about my mother?"

"Can you tell her about your dad?"

"She wouldn't believe me."

"Well, if he is a drunk, she might."

"He said he stopped drinking. After all, he is an important man in our small town. He can't let any of this get out."

"Let's hope he tells your mother so you can go home to loving parents. You must finish school and then you can go away to college or work. It will be hard living at home with him but you are a bright girl."

Kate went back to her room. I called in my three administrators. After all, we were Kate's support group and prayer team.

CORA

I finally ordered an air conditioner for my apartment. I paid $500 for it; $50 down and will pay $25 a month for two years. It felt so good.

In July we had a dinner in the park for the patients. It was warm for me to leave my eighty-degree apartment but it was cooler for the patients. Cecil made a wonderful meal of fried chicken, potato salad and baked beans. We had watermelon for dessert. Lyle had set up tables with table cloths but we used paper plates.

The dumb waiter was busy going up and down for a long while to get everything up there. My blood pressure was so high that day. It was in the 200's.

Mrs. McEwen, Mrs. Dysart and Mrs. Lowe and I sat at different tables with the girls. They were so cute the way they talked of their families and most were eager to go home to them. Of course Kate wasn't. But she was young and would adapt just fine.

We were just sitting around, some on the swing and some on a glider so full after our meal when one of the girls, who was like a little imp in her joking ways, came out to the park with bunny ears. Everyone got quiet. The young girl thought it was funny and pranced around with them wiggling. I saw Nancy get red in the face. She said, "Give those to me."

Gretchen, the young girl laughed and said, "Make me."

Nancy got up to take them from her and tried to run after her. Of course she couldn't run but she was walking very fast. She finally got them and went inside.

Mrs. Lowe, Mrs. Dysart and I looked at each other and Mrs. McEwen came over to me and said, "Was Nancy a Playboy Bunny?"

"That would explain why she wants so many massages and is afraid of stretch marks on her breasts," I said.

I called Gretchen over to me and she ambled over with her head down. "Did you go into her private room, Gretchen, and take those? And were they out in plain sight?"

"Yes, Mrs. Haworth, I saw the cleaning lady see that something was sticking out of her dresser drawer and she opened it to put it back in. I noticed it looked like a furry ear so when she was gone, I went in to look. I thought they were cute. I don't know why she has such a thing, nor why she would be so upset."

I gave her a scolding and told her never to go into anyone's private room without being invited. And she should never do anything like that with a roommate's things either.

I went in to Nancy's room and she was crying. I said, "Nancy, I scolded Gretchen. She really didn't know what she had but thought they were cute. She saw the cleaning lady notice an ear was sticking out of your drawer and she opened it to put it back. Gretchen went in later to see what it was. It looked so interesting to her. Please don't be upset. Are you a Playboy Bunny? Is that why you want so many massages?"

"Yes, I didn't want anyone to know. I feel so horrible but it pays so well and I have only one more year of college. My family doesn't even know what my job has been."

"It's nothing to be ashamed of, Nancy. You have or had the figure for it and you will have it again in a couple of months. No one needs to know. Gretchen didn't figure it out."

"Well, the others may figure it out. I haven't let anyone come in to my room and now they will know why."

"I'm guessing you got pregnant by one of the customers?"

"Yes, she cried. I didn't know he was married. We are not supposed to go out with any customer so that was my mistake."

"What if I told you that my daughter has been to a Playboy club here in Kansas City with her husband and even took their children? They just had dinner. It's nothing to be ashamed of. I almost went with them."

"Oh, Mrs. Haworth, you did? Thank you so much for sharing that."

I left her and went back to my cool apartment. It was a long day. I wished I had air conditioners for the entire hospital.

TRUDY

That picnic was something else. Several of us guessed Nancy was a Playboy Bunny, the way she carried on when she saw Gretchen wearing the ears. That day I walked in on her she had a fur thing she put away. It must have been the tail.

I was getting close to having the baby and hadn't heard from Frank so I thought I'd tell Mrs. Haworth I would give the baby up for adoption. I was tired of not being able to sleep wondering what to do and I thought I'd feel better making a decision. I wished I had a roommate I could talk to but Kate was too young to understand and she had enough problems of her own. I didn't even know how to help her. She said Mrs. Haworth had made her feel better.

I'd been listening to the girls tell their stories about how their parents reacted when they heard of their pregnancies. Some of the girls had planned to marry the father but the parents wouldn't allow it. I couldn't believe the parents wouldn't want to have a grandchild. How could they have given up such a joy? My parents would have loved for me to keep the baby but they thought it was Frank's. I just couldn't tell them my slip-up. They would have been shocked.

Some of the parents were so angry at their daughters, they didn't even correspond. The girls felt abandoned. I felt so badly for them. We went to the church service in the library on Sundays but I can't say I heard much about being forgiven. We were all sinners but God forgave us, especially if we repented.

The fathers of the babies, the responsible parties, didn't seem to get punished at all. They still had friends and went on with their lives. Why is there a double standard? I thought I might go back to school to study psychology or something similar. There was so much to learn about people.

Yes, I now felt better making a decision to give up the child for adoption. I still had hopes to marry Frank when he came home from the war.

CORA

Finally an attractive maternity outfit was designed and it was called Page Boy. All of the girls wanted to go shopping for one so cabs were called and they went downtown to a department store to try some on. Some girls ordered them from mail-order catalogs. The secret was the scooped-out window in front of the skirt which accommodated the expanding stomach. The shirt was long enough to cover the window. When patterns were made available, some of the girls made their own in our sewing room. All the staff were happy to see these new outfits appear in the cafeteria and around the halls.

Here is an excerpt from an article published in the Sunday Tribune once the Juvenile Court took over adoptions.

> *The adoption court in Kansas City places about 1,000 babies a year, thus making it one of the largest and possibly THE largest child placement agency in America. In contrast to the scores of orphanages, maternity homes, hospitals and other institutions or homes from which children may be adopted in most cities, Kansas*

City has only four. They are the Eastside, Fairmount, and Willows hospitals -- maternity homes exclusively for unwed mothers; and the Florence Crittenton Home for Infants.

Any applications that are sent direct to the maternity homes are automatically referred to the adoption department of the Juvenile court. The court's own caseworkers make all the investigations and recommendations for placement. There is only one adoption agency (the court), one adoption Judge (Ray G. Cowan), and one adoption director (Mary Lowe Fenberg) whose recommendation to Judge Cowan is required in every adoption proceeding. There are fifteen staff members under Mrs. Fenberg who are assigned to the adoption office to interview adoptive parents and unwed mothers. The others are full time case workers who are assigned to the four maternity hospitals to investigate the background of both the mothers and fathers of the illegitimate children, and to check on the health and physical development of the babies. The Kansas City adoption court has become nationally famous for its job of matching babies to parents.

Qualifications for adoptive parents are high. The theory is that with nearly 100 applicants for every available baby, the agency can be choosy. Wealth is not a prerequisite, though the court requires that applicants offer proof of enough financial security to provide comfortable standards of living and education for the child. Also, couples who want a Kansas City baby must be regular church goers. Just belonging to a church isn't enough.

Unfortunate girls who can't afford to pay for their confinement and care are usually referred to the Crittenton Home, but for the most part, those who enter the other three hospitals are girls and women from respectable family backgrounds.

It's no secret that I had not been happy with their taking over placement. I liked doing it myself. I was more cautious about where and with whom the babies were placed.

EPILOGUE 1952, 1953

EPILOGUE, 1952, 1953 -

The last two years of Cora's life were penned daily in her five-year diary. She suffered from headaches and had surgery for glaucoma. She had a lot of dizziness. She was in the hospital the month of April 1953 with high blood pressure 290/140. Her doctor Engel was worried about her and told her to keep very quiet.

However business was very slow. She borrowed $1,000.00 from Lyle, the maintenance man, to make payroll for everyone but herself. Lyle and Ole were about eighty years old and still working hard as they had all those years. Peg helped by borrowing $500 from the bank to keep the hospital going.

Her housekeeper got drunk and left.

"The nurses wanted too much money," she wrote.

Her family from Independence, Kansas, Ruthie and Fred and children came often to see her as she complained of being so lonely. Her son, Don and Peg and Carol lived in town and were busy buying a smaller home. She worried about that.

She and EP celebrated their fiftieth wedding anniversary at the Town House in Kansas City, Kansas where her sister, Virginia, worked and the whole family was there.

She spent the forty-seventh anniversary of the hospital alone as EP was in New York City.

She held a grand dinner for the patients to celebrate the hospital's forty-eighth anniversary and was given an orchid by the employees.

She bought a new GE washing machine and dryer to match at Duff and Repps.

She knitted ties for her favorite TV host, Arthur Godfrey. She also knitted ties for the doctors. She made dish towels for her granddaughter, Bevy, for her hope chest. Granddaughter Carol helped her select the embroidery which she said was fun.

Cora stayed very busy. She continued to go to the Sunshine Club for evening meetings but mentioned she was so tired she could cry. "I can't stand crowds and a lot of talking. I'm too nervous." She went to the beauty shoppe weekly.

She was thrilled when two patients came in and she took in $800.00. They were few and far between.

She wrote that she went from 143 pounds to 128 the past year.

Some doctors wanted her to lease them the hospital. Her response was Gee Whiz.

She worried daily about business. She bought a new delivery table for $150.00.

Three patients left for the Florence Crittenton charity home. So sad.

On her birthday, Don and Peg had her and EP to a lovely dinner.

She bought a new sterilizer and had the smaller one repaired. She bought a big new light for the delivery room.

Her doctor wanted her to get away so she wouldn't worry about business or the lack of it. She went to Independence, Kansas to stay with Ruthie and family but a week was too much. She had to go back home.

She had her son-in-law Fred come to help her with a price to ask for the hospital. He was an accountant and had audited her books for years. They came up with $250,000 as a fair price. She showed the hospital to some Italian doctors who were looking to buy a hospital.

"Peg and I had fun talking about what we would do if I sold the hospital."

Cora enjoyed seeing General Eisenhower at the Town House. He spoke there. She sure hoped he got in as President.

She had painters paint the pergola and fences in the park.

Apparently the nurses home was made in to an old folks home which she mentioned she closed in 1953. She said she missed the nurses.

She was able to get two more nurses and the housekeeper came back.

She started getting a social security check for $78.40 a month.

She still missed her daughter, Lucille. So many things reminded her of Lucille. She said she will never get over her death two years ago.

She got a new patient and $700.00 -- a god send, she noted.

"Nurses hard to handle today. I can't do anything on account of my eyes."

"Bevy and her boyfriend Bill and my sister were here a while. Bev left to go back to Christian College and Bill went back to KU. Virginia went back to the Town House."

Near Thanksgiving time she drove to Lawrence, Kansas with Peg and Cora bought a new coat and dress.

Cora was in touch regularly with her sister Lena by phone and brother Jack who came to visit and of course her sister, Virginia.

EP came by periodically.

She listed the hospital with a realtor and hoped it would sell in ninety days.

She kept busy wrapping Christmas presents and addressing cards.

"Have trouble with the nurses again. They are so hard to handle."

She enjoyed going to lunch some days at the department stores like Emery Byrds, Macys and Peck and Peck.

Actually she did a lot of entertaining with luncheons and dinners for family and friends the whole month of December. EP came for dinner.

On December 24, 1953, she wrote, "Last day before Christmas. Presents are all tied up. Cecil made cookies. I got a blow torch today. Got so many lovely cards."

Cora May Haworth died of a heart attack that night at age 77, exactly fifty years from the night of the Maddox Home fire.

EP died of cancer in 1960 at age eighty-five.

The following letter was written by hand to Dr. Engel entitled Christmas 1953.

> Dear Dr. Engel,
>
> The Haworth family has appreciated your marrying with us the past year. Your wonderful skilled doctors, your always ready sweet nurses and you. God bless you all. You are next to Eisenhower with us. I hope these gifts I made for my favorite hardworking nurses and doctors will be just what you want. The 17,640 stitches were all a pleasure to do for each of you.
>
> A Very Merry Christmas.
>
> Cora Haworth

Her daughter-in-law, Garnet "Peggy" Haworth, continued to run the hospital until it closed in 1969.

PART THREE

THE BIRTH RECORDS

THE BIRTH RECORDS

What happened to the records?

From a June 22, 1975 Kansas City Star article, "Adopted Seek Birth Secrets" written by Bleys W. Rose:

As anyone who follows media coverage of political campaigns knows, the echo chamber around a story sometimes drowns out the facts. The truth however has a way of rising to the surface.

Below are two articles I published in 2003 regarding the likelihood of the burning pile of records. The story relies heavily on the testimony of one woman Miss Margaret Anderson, at the time a Tulsa resident who was born at the Willows in 1925. Margaret Anderson was the name on the original birth certificate of Mrs. Robert Wheeler.

The K.C. Star's Bleys W. Rose also quotes Robert Gregory, the then administrative assistant in the Kansas City Bureau of Vital Statistics. The story reported that he "doubts the records would have been much use. The best of our information indicated that they contained medical data and were of little interest to us back then."

This is the only person to refute Miss Anderson/Mrs. Wheeler's claims of the basement full of records. Were there no laws in 1969 dealing with the disposal of medical records? Just what was the "best of our information" referring to according to Mrs. Gregory? Why didn't the K.C. Star reporter do the math on the amount of paper 25,000 to 35,000 person's medical records would generate in a backyard fire and quote somebody from the K.C. Fire Department?

Miss Anderson/Mrs. Wheeler generated a bit of press coverage for herself and her organization back in 1975. Perhaps it assisted some people in obtaining their original birth certificate. Perhaps it even helped to change public attitudes toward Missouri's closed adoption laws. One thing the coverage, especially the June 2, 1975 article, did do for certain was muddy the waters of what happened in the final days of the Willows Maternity Sanitarium's operation.

Records Fire Update

Originally published 25 September 2003

In my interview with Don Stein, Fire Marshal of the K.C. Fire Department, Fire Prevention Division on September 5, he informed me that by law, the Fire Department only needs to keep fire records for five years. After that time they are destroyed due to the sheer volume of paper that is unrealistic to keep in storage. In 1975, the records system was converted from paper to a computerized system.

At the Kansas City Fire Museum, there are specially constructed ledgers that contain single line entries for fires. Chuck Gabart, a retired Kansas City MO Firefighter, who volunteers at the museum, conducted an extensive search of these ledgers for any record of a fire at 2929 Main Street, the Willows Hospital. "We were unable to find any occurrences of fires that could be remotely connected to the hospital or the destruction of records," said Mr. Gabert in an email.

"We searched the records from January 1, 1969 to June 31, 1969," continued Gabert. "I have emailed 242 retired KCFD retirees, most of which were on the department during this time, with no response to a recollection of fires in or on the premises of the Willows. I must conclude that there was no fire of any magnitude during this period."

There is a possibility that the fire may have occurred sometime after the proposed closing date of June 15, 1969, as indicated in news reports from that time. Neither the exact closing date of The Willows nor the date of the alleged fire is known.

Mr. Gabert also mentioned another option. "After our search of the records, Ray Elder the museum historian and I discussed the possible destruction of the records in question. It is likely that the hospital had an incinerator of sufficient size to dispose of the records in a reasonable length of time. If in fact they were disposed of in this manner no fire company would have been called,"

In reference to Mr. Stein's statements, Mr. Gabert requested this clarification. Mr. Stein's statements, "should be tempered with the fact that he is a records clerk at the fire marshal's office with no fire or inspection experience and no knowledge of storage or disposal practices for hospitals during the period in question."

If you have any information about the alleged records fire, please leave a comment below. I am also interested in any personal accounts from First Mothers or Willows staff that may have witnessed incineration of any materials on the Willows premises during its daily operation.

Burning Questions About Willows Records

Originally published 09 September, 2003

There definitely would have been some kind of a story in the newspaper if that actually happened," claimed Don Stein, Fire Marshal of the Kansas City Fire Department, Fire Prevention Division. He was asked to speculate on the magnitude of a fire of 250 boxes of office paper. That is an estimate of the volume of paper the Willows Hospital may have generated during its period of operation.

Dan Coleman, a librarian with seven years of experience who currently works in the Kansas City, Missouri Public Library's Special Collections Department, said, "We do a lot of research for people looking for adoption records or maternity home records." As to the number of requests for information on Kansas City maternity homes he said, we get two or three per month at least." Despite Mr. Coleman's familiarity with the subject and the fact that the Library has a vertical file dedicated to the Willows Hospital, no one is aware of any contemporaneous news items mentioning a fire immediately after the 1969 closing of the facility. There was a statement in a twice-monthly column for the Kansas City Times written by a Mildred Ray, who collected buttons and postcards dated May 7, 1982 saying, "At the closing and razing of the Willows in 1969, records of its 64 years of operation were piled in the back yard and burned. It was the end of an era." "That's all I've ever heard about their records," said Mr. Coleman.

...Try more than six 40 box pallets. In an article titled, "Refuge for Unwed Mothers to Close" published on May 27, 1969 in the Kansas City Times, Mrs. Garnet M. Haworth said, "I guess 25,000 young women have come and gone since the doors opened in 1905." Assuming 50 pieces of paper per file for 25,000 women, that makes 1,250,000 pieces of paper. A ream of copy paper contains 500 sheets. A box of copy paper contains 10 reams or 5,000 sheets. The 1,250,000 pieces of paper representing the grand total of the Willows records divides up into 250 boxes of copy paper. How long would it take to burn that much paper?

"There's some possibility where the hospital was located, if there isn't anything else around it, it could have been going for hours before anybody knew there was a fire. If it was the middle of the night it could have been going for hours until anybody saw it." Fire Marshal Stein explained that the worst fires take place in the middle of the night because it takes so long before they are discovered. He went on to question the logic behind keeping that much paper on site, calling it a fire hazard. He said, "I don't know why a hospital would have that many boxes of files laying around the hospital anyway, hospitals are to treat people, not to keep paper." If the Willows did store all of its records on site, under what conditions were they stored?

The Secretary of State of Missouri Conservation Services Notes recommends proper storage furniture, careful handling, a safe location and specific environmental conditions to ensure the longevity of vital paper documents. What storage practices were employed at the Willows? It was a privately funded entity. A June 15, 1969, Kansas City Star article explained that the Haworth's refused to "accept federal aid or any other kind with strings attached." Absent government oversight, it appears that the owners and staff of the Willows did as they pleased with the records. Had they incinerated the records a bit at a time, there might be recollections of such practices from the staff or the first mothers who stayed there. If they burned all of the records at once, even a a third of the current estimate, the blaze would have attracted attention.

A third possibility of the records becoming the property of the state of Missouri is a mixed blessing. While the records may still exist, the statues governing closed adoptions in the state make it very difficult, if not impossible, to access the records.

It was also noted that there were too many records for the county to keep for 25,000 to 35,000 babies who were born there.

AUTHOR'S NOTE

When my son Jeff and his wife, Priscilla, took her mother, who was adopted from there, to meet my Aunt Peggy Haworth who ran the hospital after Grandmother died, they were told that the records were burned in the back yard after they closed because Aunt Peggy feared the courts were changing with regard to confidentiality and more harm might be done than good as a result. Therefore, she had them all destroyed in order to make sure that the promise of confidentiality would be kept in perpetuity.

Links to adoption registries:

http://www.dss.mo.gov:80/dfs/adoir.htm
http://www.willowshospital.org:80/MOCourtSearch.html

STAR MAGAZINE DECEMBER 29, 1991

Missouri sealed its adoption records in the 1930s. But a law change in 1986 gave adoptees 21 or older access to non-identifying information about their birth parents, such as physical description and religious preference. And with permission from their adoptive parents, the adoptees can petition the court to find their birth mothers and ask if they want to be contacted.

There are two local groups formed in order for adoptees to find their roots. Kansas City Adult Adoptees Organization and Connecting Adoptees Through Research and Education (CARE).

"They aren't looking for parents," research director of CARE said. "They're looking for themselves."

FROM BIRTH MOTHERS

FROM BIRTH MOTHERS *(I took the liberty to make some spelling corrections)*
FROM QUILTED HISTORY, 2005 (From the Internet)

1946 - I remember the long, long stairs from the street up to The Willows and I was scared to death. We filled out a lot of papers as to name, age, religion, the boy's name, etc. And I presume the folks paid for things. I don't remember.

I shared a large room with three other girls on the Northwest corner on the first floor. A month after I arrived I celebrated my seventeenth birthday but there was one girl there who was as young as 14 or 15. It was terrible lonely away from home and all of my family and friends.

We had a physical when we went in The Willows and were checked and questioned about our health. There was a regular routine as to meals, chore time, etc. We had to keep our rooms clean and our laundry done. Some of the girls had jobs like in the laundry or kitchen and a few privileged ones worked in the offices. I say privileged because they got to see people from the outside world.

We had a store at The Willows where we could get toothpaste, stationery, pens, paper, etc. We learned to play a lot of solitaire. I read a lot and it seems there must have been some sort of library.

I can remember laying in bed and watching the streetcars. We could see a small strip of Main Street and the lights from downtown.

There was a delivery room there in the building but if you had any trouble, they rushed you to the regular hospital. There must have been a nursery there as I got to see my baby, but he was brought to my room. He was about 3 to 5 days old and I never saw him again. I don't see now how I did it. I just had to console myself with the fact that I couldn't support him and my folks wouldn't have. I didn't want to displease my folks or I felt they wouldn't love me anymore.

Sally B, 1958 - Nearly everyone came and went via the rear entrance. I do not even remember ever seeing the front of the building. My mother and I rode the train all night on a Friday night and arrived in Kansas City mid-morning on Saturday. We took a taxi too The Willows, where we were met by Mrs. Haworth. I have heard that Mrs. Haworth often picked up girls at the airport or train station if they came in alone, as many of them did. When my mother took me to The Willows, when she picked me up to take me home after my daughter was born, and the two times she visited during my stay there, we always used taxicabs for transportation to and/or from the train station and/or hotel. Parents of prospective residents were not allowed in the residence areas, so Mrs. Haworth took me on a tour of those areas while my mother waited in her office. There were two vacancies, both semi-private rooms, with two beds, a chest of drawers, writing table and chair and closet. I chose the room that also had a wash basin. That room was $5 a week more than the room without a wash basin. I was so angry with my mother for making me go to The Willows and give up my baby instead of letting my boyfriend and me get married the way we wanted to and I felt so unable to do anything to change the situation so I decided the only way I could get back at her was to make her pay the extra $5 a week for the room with the wash basin. That was my 16 year old way of thinking. My recollection is that the cost was about $65 a week. I do not recall if there was an extra charge for the labor and delivery areas. My room was on the second floor, facing Main Street - the front of the building. It seemed like we were rather high up. I would sit at the writing table at night, listening to the radio and writing letters as the traffic flowed on Main Street below.

There were two elderly men who lived in a small building in the rear of the main building, Lyle and Ole. They carried luggage and may have done light maintenance work as well.

There was a registered nurse, Mrs. Zukowsky (sp?) who had two small girls, probably about 3 and 5 who lived on the premises. Everyone referred to her as Mrs. Z. There were several other nurses who worked labor and delivery and the nursery, Miss Skeleton and Mrs. Ruby McClelland are the two names I remember. I developed a "relationship" with Mrs. McClelland and would often walk up the stairs to the third floor nursery to visit with her; she worked the second shift.

At the foot of the stairs leading to the nursery was a pay telephone - Valentine 1-9723. When the phone rang, the on duty nurse would come down from the nursery and answer it. The number was not listed anywhere and was considered to be secure - if someone called and asked for one of the residents, the nurse would page her. There was no limitation on the amount of time we were allowed to talk on the phone or on the frequency with which we could make or receive calls - we just had to have enough change to feed the phone.

Privacy of the residents of The Willows was a high priority. If anyone came to the door or called the telephone number listed in the phone book for The Willows, they were told no one by the name of the person they were asking for was known to them.

The mail was handled in a similar fashion. Most of the women who received mail did so under a pseudonym. The other option was to pay Mrs. Haworth an additional $20 and have mail sent to her house, obviously a residence. In that way, anyone checking would be more likely to believe that the resident was staying with her "aunt" due to illness, as was the story told by so many families to explain our absence from home. I received mail at Mrs. Haworth's home under my real name. I received my home town newspaper as another name at The Willows.

I would guess there were about 40 women there during my stay. I understand that in prior years the facility was much more crowded. Our semi-private rooms were not spacious by any means, but were comfortable for two people. There were also several private rooms on the second floor where my room was located. On the first floor there were a number of rooms with 3 and 4 beds and the scuttlebutt had it that those rooms were for girls whose parents didn't have much money. Don't know if that was so, or just gossip.

We were able to move around through the home at will. Not only did we visit each other's rooms, we could visit girls on the other floor from the one we lived on. Each floor had a TV room and I don't recall that there were any restrictions. I did not spend much time watching TV. I learned to play many variations of solitaire, worked jigsaw puzzles and visited a lot with many of the women. There was no lights out time. I'm sure if anyone had been noisy or rowdy, the nurse would have stepped in, but that never happened while I was there.

Sally, 1962 - (Contributed by Mike on behalf of someone else) The Willows was supposed to be the "elite" of maternity homes in that era. My father sent me there all the way from Tennessee when I became pregnant in 1961. I was not a willing participant in giving up my son but it was clear that I had no other choice available to me at the time. I was there from mid-November 1961 through March 26, 1962.

The attending physician at the time was Dr. Robert Slickman and he is the Dr. listed on my son's amended birth certificate... about the only info on it that is true.

We were told to pick...or have those in charge pick...a "name" to use while at The Willows...I became "Sally"...I think Mrs. Haworth picked it for me since they did not have a Sally there currently. That was one of the more unusual aspects of being there - actually having your identity stripped away. I was called Sally and received my mail from my parents addressed to Sally. I honestly think that that part of it has potential to damage one's psyche. I only knew one other girl's true first and last names and she knew mine. Of course when the time came to sign the relinquishment papers, we had to sign our legal, true name.

There were probably 20 to 30 women there during my stay at any given time. We were housed on two floors as I remember, two to a room, except it seems at the end of the floor was a private room for only one. We shared one and 1/2 baths per floor. It was a very old building; the labor/delivery rooms were on an upper floor, along with the nursery (possibly a third floor). The kitchen and dining area were in the basement and the activity/tv room was a central gathering place. Once we delivered were housed on a separate floor from the other residents.

There was a common dining hall on the lower level, basement I think. We went through sort of a cafeteria line with our trays. Of course we did not have a selection. Breakfast was usually oatmeal and toast. Lunch was soup and sandwich and for dinner we had a meat with vegetables. We passed the time doing needlework, watching tv, playing cards, painting and just talking and visiting. I don't remember us talking about anything too deeply regarding our conditions and the circumstances surrounding it.

Our ex-lovers, boyfriends, we referred to as RP's, responsible party. There was a small walking track in the back yard we could walk outside each day if the weather was nice enough. There were only two or three others that I got to know quite well. I had a couple of different roomies while there. First one left to go live with a relative and said she was keeping her child. Then I had a girl younger than I the rest of the time. She was quite unpleasant and we did not gel very well.

My closest comrade was a girl from Illinois who was due about a month after me. She and I stayed in touch for a while after I left but over the years lost touch and I do not know where she is now.

I always assumed that the adoptive parents came to The Willows and picked up their adoptee. My son's parents came from Kansas. We were never allowed in the main office area where I assumed the parents came to get a child. I worked in a small office typing envelopes to Doctors all over the country and stuffing them with a Willows brochure. We were paid a small amount of money for our work. Some of the girls even worked in the nursery and some in the laundry.

I was given NO information about the adoptee parents. Nothing was mentioned about my rights to contact him in the future. At that time I just assumed that it was a done deal and that I no longer had any rights to him. I was also given no counseling and told that in time I would get over all this and go on to have other children, which I did (two other sons) but you cannot replace the one that was lost to adoption. The getting over it is a myth. I have met and been in contact with many birth moms over the years and have yet to meet one that simply got over it.

As far as your statement about admiration for our strength and courage, this is a comment that I have heard from others since I came out with my story. In most cases this is a myth. It was neither strength or courage. It was in most cases coercion and even a forced situation. These young women of that era had no resources. Unwed motherhood was practically a crime. We would have had a very difficult time obtaining a job enabling us to support our child. Most had families that totally refused to help them in any way. It was a desperate situation. We were made to feel that it would be very selfish to keep our child and if we loved them we would give them up to a better life.

I think most of use who were confined to the homes of that era felt for the most part that we were doing time, our crime of falling in love with the wrong guy. All stories are different though and some of the girls had even had an offer of marriage but for whatever reason chose this course. At times it seems like this did not really happen to me, but to someone else, even after eleven years it seems surreal.

Sandy, 1965-66 - I just have to get all my thoughts together and figure out how to present the "story." To tell you the truth, I've never said a word to anyone about being there. My husband and children know I was there but they have never asked what it was like or anything concerning that time so I haven't ever verbalized on it. I may do this in segments if you don't mind. Mrs. Haworth, a very proper gray haired and stout lady met my Mother and me at the airport to take us to the Willows. She seemed to chat about rules and activities all the way to the home. She asked my name and I was told there was already a Nancy there so my name from that moment on was Sandy. All communication was to Sandy Haworth and everyone there only knew me by that name.

We pulled up to the back of The Willows, entered the back door and went straight to her office for as it turned out, she was the owner. I was asked if I wanted a private or double room. Other than that all conversation was with my Mother. Mrs. H called a taxi to come for Mom and when it arrived, against protest from Mrs. H., I escorted her out the front door, around back to the cab and said my good-byes. After getting a tongue lashing from Mrs. H, I was shown upstairs to my room, a room I made home for 6 months.

The room was pleasant enough if not a bit old fashioned, with twin beds, a free standing closet that was 4'X 2' and 6' tall, mirror, sink, dresser and area rug between the beds. My room was on the third story facing the main street. I say the third floor because we lived, basically on three floors. The basement served as the first floor and where we went for all of our meals. The second floor, or main floor, had dorm rooms with a maximum of two to a room and the offices. The third floor had dorm rooms, a TV room, the clinic, labor, delivery and recovery rooms. The fourth floor had the babies. There was an enclosed yard on the south where we walked if we wanted and most of us did. So many times around the perimeter equaled a mile and in all kinds of weather we tried.

I settled in to my room, got my bearings, and started in on the daily living at The Willows. It seems like it was a couple of days when the social worker came to talk to me about the adoption. You were right about the non-counseling. There was no talk of alternatives; it was just questions about my social and medical history and the father's. I never saw her again for any talk until after Chad was born.

We learned not to get too excited about mealtime. They were generally pretty bad, nutritious, but bland as no salt or seasonings were used. That was to keep our weight gain down, as the goal was for us to leave not looking like he had had a baby. It wasn't unusual for us to skip a meal now and then and they didn't worry about that unless we missed too many in a row. One girl did that and the meals started showing up in her room. I rarely had breakfast, always oversleeping until mail call. That woke me up.

Mail call was every morning about the same time. Mrs. H would read off all our first names over the intercom and we would go down to her office area to pick up our mail. All the letters were sent to our "given" names with her last name. Mine were addressed to Sandy Haworth. Sometimes packages would arrive with treats and they were certainly gobbled up quickly.

After a short time I asked if I could work in the nursery. They only used us if we volunteered and would pay us $2.00 a day for it. I don't know if I ever actually got paid since the money was to be taken off my bill. I do remember that I was the only one at the time to work up there.

The nursery was on the very top floor. It was sunny and bright and the babies were so eager to have even a little bit of attention and love. We would keep them all snuggled in their little bassinets, prop a bottle for them so they could get fed.

It was impossible to hold each one to feed them but we would pick them up for burping. They usually were adopted out within a few months but I do remember feeling very sorry for one little boy who was there for almost a year. One of the nurses said they had a child there for almost two years, but that was very rare.

They did have toys and a playpen for the little boy and he seemed quite content. I didn't work every day but they would call me on the intercom when they needed me, usually in the mornings, waking me up. I was always happy to see an empty crib for I knew another baby went "home." The last month I didn't work. I got too big to get around the bassinets easily. I missed seeing all those little faces look up and smile to me.

The rest of the day was spent reading, gossiping, watching TV, playing cards, walking and I did some crafts that I had brought with me. When I ran out of those, I'd go to the department store downtown and get some more.

Yes, we were allowed to go shopping one day a week. We'd usually go in at least pairs if not in groups. We'd put on our wedding bands that we bought at a dime store, call for a cab and go, usually to the Hallmark Mall. I preferred to go downtown to the older, big stores since there I could find bookstores and sewing craft projects to buy. One thing for sure - we always ate something out. It seems to me that some of the Catholic girls went to church on Sundays, but since I'm not Catholic, I didn't pay too much attention to that. That may have been just during the holidays.

What were the girls like? I only had one roommate the entire time I was there and she was there just 1 1/2 months. She came in not looking like she was pregnant then, boom, she relaxed and she was 8 months along. She was from New Jersey. We had a good time together - lots of laughs. One time we re-arranged the furniture in our room and got reprimanded for it, but we liked it. It stayed that way until she went into labor then the housekeepers put it back their way.

Another girl was from Minnesota and really rich. She stayed in her room most of the time but was fun. We all gathered in her room to play cards and talk. Her boyfriend came for a visit, took her out shopping and for meals. Another girl was from Chicago and had been a Playboy Bunny.

I remember the 14-year-old chubby girl from Tennessee who never looked pregnant and didn't change even after she delivered. There was a school teacher. But most of us were college girls from middle class families.

Most of the girls wore clothing that had been left there from past girls. I was lucky in that my mother came for a visit and took me shopping for some so I didn't have to wear hand-me-downs.

A doctor regularly visited us in the clinic. They would call our names over the intercom to go to the clinic to be checked out. Of course, the further along we were the more often we'd go.

The labor, delivery and clinic rooms were on the same floor and were only towards the back of the building. It must have been pretty sound proof as I don't remember ever hearing anyone in pain. I don't remember ever hearing of any c-sections but surely they had some.

After we delivered we went to the recovery area for a few days before going home. All of our belongings would already be there. The other girls would come to visit to see how it all went and marvel at how thin we were and well we looked. The bad food paid off.

We were allowed to see our child for about an hour, only once, to hold him and give him a lifetime of love - just one hour.

The social worker came again to take us to court. We really didn't talk much about the proceedings on the way there. It would have been nice to know what it was going to be like.

We would sit at a large table with men and women around it asking us questions as to why we were giving up our child. Through questions, I think, in retrospect, it didn't matter what we said since it was pretty much a "done deal." This was just a formality. We signed the papers and went back to the home.

The social worker did ask if we wanted to know anything about the people who adopted our baby - of course I did!!! She would write and let us know. I got a letter about a month later about the a-parents. Funny how it sounded just like the one another girl had written to me that she got. Hmmmmmmm.

My parents arrived the next day to take me to a spa for a couple of days then back home.

Have I tried finding Chad? Not really. I just recently sent the state of Missouri my consent form and I will let it sit there. If he wants to find me he is welcome to but I won't interfere in his life if he doesn't want it.

I feel very strongly that the birthparent does not have the right to search out the child. We freely gave up that right when we signed the papers. Of course I want to know all about him, how he turned out, what type of person he is, what type of life he has had, is he happy. I ache every day not knowing, BUT I don't have that right to know.

His parents took him in with faith that he was their child and I wouldn't interfere and I have to respect their rights. Chad didn't sign away his rights to know me and therefore, if he ever wants to search me out, I will gladly and willingly be available to him. It is only a very selfish person who searches for the child they gave up. (I know I'm probably not "politically correct" for these times but that is the way I feel.)

I was there from the first part of October to the first part of April. I was one of the longer stayers. It was a bit strange to me because my parents wanted to hide me as fast as possible when they found I was pregnant.

I believe that in the early days there used to be some big Willow trees in the front of the building. Don't know where I'm pulling that from - maybe a guess or an old faded memory.

I don't remember that Christmas was much unlike any other day except that we had a nicer meal and watched Christmas programs on the TV. We didn't decorate except to put Christmas cards around our rooms, didn't sing carols. I honestly don't remember if Mrs. H showed up at Christmas but she may have. She would opt in from time to time to say a friendly hello. I'm thinking her office area and front hall, where adoptive parents would go, had a bit of decorating but I don't remember anything else being decorated.

We only had, that I know of, one Jewish girl at that time and I have no idea if she celebrated Hanukah.

No, there were no black women having babies. I believe there was a black housekeeper and she was a very nice lady.

On the Northeast corner of the parking lot, which was on the east side of the building, I remember a structure that was the incinerator. I remember it because on the days I would go shopping, the cab would always pick us up on that side of the building and the trash would be burning.

You mention that in talking to birth mothers, they have told you of "colossal" shame. Isn't that a sad commentary on the society of the time? I don't think we ever discussed being ashamed while at the home. Perhaps some did but I wasn't included in those discussions because they all knew that my pregnancy was the result of a date rape situation. I felt shame. Society back then didn't believe in date rape or even rape, for that matter, so the shame and guilt had to be mine. My own parents would never discuss it with me and I am sure, even in their elderly years before passing away, they didn't believe in it. I was given a choice, at the time, of an illegal abortion or The Willows and I chose life.

Being that I am in a unique position of being adopted myself and giving a cild up for adoption I can understand many sides to the adoption triad. I feel that because of my situation it was probably easier to give Chad up than it was for many of the girls who genuinely loved their child's father. Some went home to wedding plans, after all. I went with one girl who picked out her wedding dress and bought it.

I wasn't embittered toward Chad, at all. I knew there was a purpose for him being there or the whole thing wouldn't have happened. I guess that's my Christian faith coming out in me. Also, being that I had been adopted by wonderful people, I felt that he would be also, and I've always prayed that was so.

You could think of us as a bunch of girls living in a college dorm spending time chatting with each other, reading, having meals together, playing cards, doing crafts, shopping together. We just were all pregnant and there for one reason. Our attitude wasn't doom and gloom - we had some very fun times together and some good laughs.

Society was very different back then. I know that social workers did their very best in trying to match babies with parents. My parents went through a yearlong screening process before they could get me. It was that way for my brother too. Every adopted parents, from those days, who I have talked to said it was a frightening experience because they knew that just one little thing wrong could keep them from having a child. And I'm talking about a little thing like having a messy room during a surprise inspection, or having a friend that a social worker didn't like.

I feel that The Willow's social worker did her best. She just didn't want to take the time to write letters to each of us so she made up a form. Oh well, if she had written to each of us she might have inadvertently told us something that could lead to identifying the parent. It's all right. It really is. It just wasn't too ethical.

I hope this has helped you understand life at The Willows and that you can relate this to anyone asking. It wasn't a prison and we formed bonds with each other. We cared about each other. We never corresponded with each other. We never knew our last names. The nurses and the housekeepers were all very nice to us. I do feel sad that such institutions aren't around like that anymore. Oh, there are a very few but abortion or keeping the baby seems to be the way now. There are so many couples wanting babies and it was a good source for them.

FROM LETTERS TO MRS. NICHOLS, THE SOCIAL WORKER. THESE ARE FROM MISSOURI STATE HISTORICAL SOCIETY

> 5-5-65 - I want to thank you ever so much for writing me about my baby. I was so relieved to know of his home at last and his new family, even including a brother! I would say that fortune is with him though I wish I were too.
>
> I also thank you for your best wish for Duane and me and as you know however, that he and I have separated at long last under my direction. I have had no word from him as he played one too many heartless tricks on me. I would have married him, my friend, for the reason that Terry was his son and no other man would want my own in my condition. And I could have made him a good wife but not loving for all of my love was crushed by him after I got home. I know he's very likable at first meeting! But it's the other meetings that really count. Well, God has been good to me and let me return to the one I wrote all the time to a while in Kansas. He's Arabic, not even a citizen, 24 and the one I ached for in place of Duane. In April we were married & the day before our marriage news of Terry came. I think we are meant to be together. He has known about my misfortune all along and holds nothing against me. Everything

from here on counts. We are so happy & I'm at last satisfied with life and the one I love. Life couldn't have turned out better for me.

I've written because I wished you to know my fortune to boost others' morals with, if possible. My regards to you, Miss Lowell, & Mrs. Haworth. Your outlook is so healthy on us.

Thanks for everything and putting my mind at ease at last, and Terry in comfort & love.

5-14-1966 - Dear Mrs. Nichols, I have thought about writing to you for many months but have always talked myself out of it but tonight I have so many memories that they simply cannot be contained.

I have so many memories. I am getting ready to graduate now. The big day will be May 29. I'm looking forward to it for it has been a long awaited for day. Now that it's so near I'm scared. I've had to pick up and start over too many times that it's hard to have to do it again so soon. I have my job all lined up, however I will be a social caseworker beginning June 20. I'm looking forward to it but I'm a little worried. Did you believe when I was there that year that I'd ever make it?

This has been a difficult year for me. You probably won't be able to recall my case but I was engaged before going to The Willows. While there I shut ——————- out completely because he had not been responsible for my being there and I didn't want him to share all the heartache. Well, after coming home I was ready to pick up our relationship again but then he was not. Needless to say, that was hard because I felt that I had lost everything and wished I could have died. I came back to school in September and was very miserable the first semester. But, I'm becoming my old self again except for this month. It's practically, as though, I were experiencing the same thing all over again.

I would give anything if I knew how to contact ——— ———. Has she written to you? If she has, would you write to her and ask her to write to me? An experience such as that is one that can never be forgotten and relationships are never forgotten either.

Well, I am addressing my announcement now so I'll send one to you too. I know you are very busy but if you could contact ——————, I'd be very grateful.

There are, of course, many questions I'd like to ask you about but I don't want to put you on the spot. If there is anything you can tell me though I would be pleased.

Thank you for your kindness. Please remember me to Mrs. Kraemer. I would write to her but I hesitate.

As ever,

Hi Joan, I'm sure you don't remember me too well but I remember you and how thoughtful you were. All is well and I'm enjoying the area I am working and living in. I often think of The Willows and of course of the little one and how she is fairing but that is all. If you still work for Mrs. Haworth, please give her my best and do write when you can and I'd love to hear from you.

Sincerely,

May 6, 1965 - Dear Mrs. Nichols, I was very happy to get your letter about Mark and I know in the years to come he will be too.

Well, everything with me has been great. You should hear some of the stories about Kansas City I have made up to explain three months. Oh, brother. I have been looking for a job ever since I came home from ——————.

But haven't had much luck. We are moving into our new home so that has kept me pretty busy.

As for ——————————, I have gone out with him once since I have been home and I know it will never work out between us ever again. Unless the service does something for him. He leaves the first of July. In a way I am glad because it is pretty hard on me to see him and think about ——————————. I have been dating a few guys that I went to school with and I guess in a way starting all over again.

You might think this is a little dumb but could you or should I say will you please send me a picture of your son that is a senior this year. One of his senior pictures. My girl friend thinks it's a little funny I don't have any pictures. If you rather not I'll understand.

Guess I better go for now. Thanks again for your letter and write when you get a chance.

Love,

P.S. Say hi to all the nurses and Mrs. Haworth for me.

Anonymous - Panic gripped me. I didn't know what to do. I was very much pregnant and very much unmarried. I had trusted Dave. He loved me so he said. After eight months of refusing him, I had finally given in. I was so in love and so stupid. Surely he would take care of me if anything went wrong. He was a respectable lawyer and budding politician at 35. Surely, when I told him he would marry me and make everything all right. Oh my brave Fiorello, my crusader for man's rights. What a fool you made of me! He refused to marry me, refused to help me at all, refused to take any of the blame, said it was all my fault. It is bad enough to lose the man you're crazy about but to love him when you need him so desperately is nearly fatal. What could I do now?

How could I tell my parents? I was their pride, a prosperous business woman at 24, a respected member of the community following in my father's footsteps. Everyone in our large metropolitan community remembers Dad's days in public office. He helped make our city what it is today. How could I bring such disgrace on his name? Suicide seemed the only answer, a death that looked like an accident. I drove my car up and down Riverside Drive trying to get the nerve to plunge it over the cliff. I couldn't. I had committed one terrible sin. Committing another would not make things right. I told my folks that night.

I never realized until that night what truly great people my parents were. It was a terrible shock to them and they first scolded me roundly. I was grateful for that. I not only deserved it but needed it. It showed how much they loved me. Within a week, Dad had accepted my plight and even tried to cheer me up. He joked, "Don't feel so bad. Remember, this isn't the only one." I was instructed to never see Dave again. If he would not marry me, he had no right to ever know what happened from then on. We agreed that abortion was not the answer. It was illegal and dangerous. We also agreed that no one else must find out if I was to continue working in our community. The only answer was to get out of town and find a respectable home where both the baby and I would be in good hands. I couldn't stay in one of the many homes in town because too many of my parents friends worked on their boards and volunteer staffs. I tried the homes in Florida because my parents would be vacationing there for two months. But they were all controlled by the state and would not take out-of-state patients. Oh, were they rude on the phone. Their voices condemned me. I felt sorry for the girls in their charge. I thought of trying the other cities in my state, but my parents vetoed it. Dad had too many contacts. I'd run too good a chance of seeing someone he knew. I tried other homes out of state but found none that seemed suitable.

Then our doctor suggested The Willows in Kansas City. He knew very little about the place except that several nice families had adopted children from there. If people came as far as 1000 miles from home to adopt, I figured it must be a reputable home, so I called. What a relief to hear a friendly voice on the other end. This person couldn't be the typical underpaid social worker just out of college with the pat prying questions, the monotone memorized replies, the underlying condemnation with superiority inflection that I had heard at the many other homes. This was a grandmotherly voice as kind and concerned for my wellbeing as my own mother's. I was not asked embarrassing questions, was filled in on exactly what it cost, what I needed to bring, what the girls were like and so on. All she asked me was my age, when I was due, if I had seen a doctor and if my parents knew. My father had been listening on another line and agreed this was the place to go. We didn't want me to go so far away, but there was no other home closer that seemed as nice. All the others were run on charity and took in, God only knows, what kind of girls. I knew if they treated the girls like they spoke to me on the phone, I would really be a mental wreck when it was over. I knew what I had done. I had condemned myself enough and did not need someone else to help me. I needed a private place where I could work things out and make my peace with God and my conscience. I called The Willows again, told them when I would arrive at the airport and what I looked like.

I was plenty scared when I got off the airplane. The unknown is always awesome. But as soon as I saw the lady waiting at the foot of the ramp, I felt at home. The stylish little woman with beautiful white hair, wearing a suit of impeccable taste, smiled, and I kew she was the lady on the phone. She looked not unlike my mother. Her husband brought the car up. It was just like our family car. I had driven to the airport with one set of parents and was driving home from another airport with another set of parents.

From that moment to this, I have been very much at home. The girls here all come from similar homes as I. We are closer friends than my own sorority in college was. I have no fear for my privacy here - no fear of being blackmailed by some girl who might, in the future, get on dope and need money. They are all nice girls who, like myself, made a mistake and who intend to never make it again. We are all one family, the girls, Mrs. Haworth and her employees, trying to help each other through this difficult time, easing our fears and guilts, and preparing us to meet the difficulties of giving away our babies and facing the world again.

I don't know what would have happened to me if I hadn't come here. I hate to think of it. I am so grateful that The Willows exists. I am paying for these six months entirely by myself with the money I saved to open my own business but it is worth it to me. I know my baby will get a good home, that my secret will stay a secret, and that I will leave here having made my peace with God and ready to face the world again.

> July 11, 1968 - Dear Mrs. Nichols, I got your letter today and I'm so glad everything is turning out so well! Thank you so much for writing me right away.
>
> I'm enclosing the two recipes you wanted. I hope you like the white chocolate cake one too!
>
> My Mom was really impressed with the nice lawyer and you and everyone around your office. (So was I of course) She thought the judge was great and I certainly appreciated all the good advice and nice things he said to me. They have been something to lean on when the going gets rough around ———. I've been seriously considering going away to school for my junior and senior years. I don't want to run away from anything - I only want to be accepted————— liked and approved of——————. It's been so long since I've been really happy.

People around here can be so cruel! I hold my head up and act like I don't hear the remarks they make but I cry myself to sleep every night. I suppose after a while they'll forget somewhat if I conduct myself respectfully and be a lady, but I wonder how long it will take?

Haven't I paid for my "crime" and haven't I "served my time" and cried billions of tears and wanted to die and hated myself for being so stupid? What do they want? Blood?

I guess I was silly to think this was over. Apparently it's only the beginning. I'm sorry for unloading my problems but I have to talk to someone. Thank you again. I hope you enjoy the recipes.

Lots of love,

Oct. 31 - Dear Mrs. Nichols, I'm sorry I've taken so long to write you back but I had a surprise visit from my ex-high school roommate whom I haven't seen in five years. We had a great visit and she stayed for two weeks.

I am so happy to hear about Deanna. Her new parents sound like wonderful people and I know she'll get the best life has to offer. Mother, Daddy and the maid who has been with us for 15 years read the letter and they too were very pleased with the way Deanna's parents sounded. I wish I could meet them, but maybe it's better that I can't.

I would like to ask one question if I may, can you tell me if her parents took the little yellow dress and booties which I bought her? I left a note with the nurses asking them to see if the parents wanted them as a present from her mother.

Everything is going fine in school. My courses aren't real hard but I still have to study a lot. My week ends are spent at the football games and so we've only lost one.

I hear from ———— often and she seems to be getting along fine. She and ———— moved into an apartment together and both have jobs. She sounds real happy.

Who all is left out of the "old" group? What did ——— ——— and ———— have and I hope everything went okay for them. Keep me posted.

By the way, did you ever get ———— straightened out? I hope so cause I felt so sorry for her baby.

Better close for now. Please give the nurses, Lottie, May, Dorothy, Mrs. Haworth, etc. my love.

Thank you for all you did for me, and a million, million thanks for taking care of my baby. I know she has the very best and will continue to have.

Write when you can. I miss you lots.

Love always,

P.S. Did you get your license plates straight? Tell your family hi.

ADOPTEES LETTERS

ADOPTEES LETTERS

FROM QUILTED HISTORY - 2005 (on the internet)

1948 - Anonymous - I was born on June 9 at the Willows. My adoptive parents came from Ft. Worth, TX to pick me up in Kansas City. They had adopted my older brother from the Willows 2 years earlier. My brother and I grew up knowing we were adopted. We heard some of the ugly words some people said about adoptees in the 1950's. My mother read us the book, The Chosen Child and I think we felt special.

After my adoptive parents passed away I began looking for my roots. My brother had no interest in searching. I contacted the state and got my non-identifying information. I was amazed to get 4 pages of information about my birth parents. I contacted a searcher with all the information I had. I did not realize that the crib card I possessed had a name that meant something.

After a few weeks I had a name to start my search. I spent a lot of time on the internet just looking. The name on the crib card was ________ which turned out to be my maternal grandmothers name. I wrote and got death certificates for both grandparents. I found the cemetery where they were buried, on the internet, and sadly to say there was my birthmother's name.

I wrote to the funeral home and got a copy of her death certificate. I was stunned by the information I was seeing. My birthmother passed away in 1976 while she and her family were living in Singapore.

The strange thing was that I lived in Singapore at the same time. There was not a large American community living in Singapore at that time…could we have seen each other?

I will never know.

I continued my search. I wrote and got the marriage certificate for my birthmother to her husband about a year after I was born. With that information I was able to find my half-brothers and sister.

Another surprise, one half brother lives in the same city in NC I live in now. He does not want any contact but I will continue to send Christmas cards in hopes of a chance to meet.

I did in fact meet my other half brother and half sister last spring. They were very kind but I am the only one to make contact. I'm sure it is very difficult to find that your mother had a secret they never knew about. I will give it time.

I am still searching for my birthfather. I have a searcher working with me for the last six months. I have a feeling that he has passed away. There has not been any luck so far. My searcher gave me a few clues to find him. I am searching on Classmates.com for anyone who knew my birthmother, old friends who may have known who she was dating. I hope to get more information in the future.

Darlene, 1949 - I was born at the Willows Oct. 15, in 1949. The name given me then was Darlene. There also was another birthdate of two days later. My mother was able to meet my first mom and was able to talk to her for a while. She was a farm girl from Nebraska who had come to the big city to work. She was swept off her feet by a young man who worked in a creamery in the area. She was 20 years old at the time and came from a very strict family who never knew of the pregnancy. I wonder about her often and hope sincerely that she has had as good of life as I've had. To find her and thank her has been a life long dream. It is made more important by the fact that I also have an adopted daughter and three other children that I would love for her to know about. Without her and the Willows and the sacrifice that she made, none of this would have been possible.

Carolyn Hunt Haney

Beverly, 1948 - I was born in an unwed mother's home in Kansas City, MO. on or about June 2, 1948. I was one of triplets. I was told that the other two babies, (girls) died at birth. I cannot locate any death records for 2 babies on that date. Then I was told that my adoptive parents couldn't take all 3 of us so we were split up. I was adopted by Burl William and Marion Francis Bryant from Excelsior Springs, MO.

I was told my biological mother was a young college student and that the biological father was a professor at the college. I don't know if it is true. I have olive skin and dark hair with hazel/brown eyes. I do not have any medical background or nationality information about myself.

Unfortunately I do not have any information about the biological parents. This small amount is all I can tell you about me. If anyone can help, I would greatly appreciate it.

Beverly Diane (Bryant) Geary.

Betty, 1928 - I was born at the Willows Maternity Sanitarium January 15, 1928, having red hair and blue eyes and weighing 7 lbs. My birth mother was a young woman from the area of Holton, KA who was a secretary to the law firm of Fairchild and Hamilton Fulton in 1927.

I am reasonably certain that Hamilton Fulton was my birth father and he subsequently became my adopted father as well, when he convinced his wife to agree to adopting me. Thus I was adopted at the age of 2 weeks by Hamilton and Opal Wells Fulton. One of the conditions of the adoption was that I would never be told of the circumstances.

Both of my adoptive parents are now dead. I currently have engaged an attorney who is bringing a lawsuit to have my original records given to me. Beyond the need to know about my birth, I would also like to publicly state my gratitude to my birth mother for giving me life.

Betty Alexander

Elle,1965 - I was born in The Willows Hospital July 6,1965. I believe that my birth name was Jennifer Chase. When I tried to find out about my birth mother from adoption organizations, I was told that my records were "burned" in a fire. My sister was also a Willows baby born in 1964.

Ellie Dare

Faye, 1936 - I was born at the Willows August 14, 1936. My name was Faye Rogers. I was adopted by John and Mildred Fisher Busch. They lived in Pleasanton, Nebraska. They had a birth son much older than I.

My adopted father had a drinking problem. When I was four years old my mother divorced him. She then married John Kenney, Jr. He had three children by his first wife who had died in childbirth.

At one point the new family moved to a little town in Iowa. It was my adopted mother, her second drunk husband, one birth child, three step-children and me. My mother had her son. My step-father had his daughter and two sons and then there was me. It was not a very nice life.

John Kenney killed himself. His oldest son killed himself. John's daughter became a school teacher, a wife and mother. The youngest son drank himself to death.

I married a wonderful man. He was a military officer so we were truly everywhere. In our family we have three sons, one daughter, six grandchildren and eight great-grandchildren.

My husband died in 2003. We were married fifty years. I found my birth mother two years ago. She was eighty-seven years old and I am sixty-seven years old. She lives in a small town close to Kansas City, MO. She has lived there her whole life.

I looked for her my whole life. She doesn't want anything to do with me. She told me in a phone conversation that those were bad times for her and she wanted to forget.

I would love to see her and put my arms around her. I would love to see pictures of her and her family. I would love to know who my father was. She will not tell me.

She was married three years after giving birth to me. She has a son that is my half brother. He won't talk to me or write to me. My mother asked me not to call her anymore.

All of my adopted family are gone now, not that we were ever close. I made a good life for myself and I have been happy. I love my God and my family that I gave birth to.

Fay Rogers Stowe

Johnathan, 1969- I've always known I was adopted. My parents told me that I was special because they got to choose me. In my baby book created by my adoptive mother, there is a baby formula booklet with the name Baby Jonathan at the top.

I wondered who my other parents were. What did they look like? Where did they live? Were they still alive? Were they artists like me?

On the day I was given to my adoptive parents, my father scribbled down some notes about my first mother and her family. Since they matched up with my non-identifying history, I relied on a clue contained in them. He had written "Iowa?" above the physical description, suggesting she could have been from there. Every time I was in Iowa, I'd stop at the library in a town and look at old year books. I would scan the faces for familiar traits. There were a few contenders but nothing definitive.

It wasn't until my older sister, also adopted, was well under way searching for her first parents that I began to think about searching for mine. In 1992 she sent away for a search book she had seen on a daytime talk show. It was very helpful in guiding her through unknown territory. This was before the explosion of information on the web.

She approached both of our adoptive parents with consent forms. Missouri law requires adult adoptees to obtain notarized consent from both adoptive parents before the first parents are located and contacted through third party. One parent agreed and the other declined. Having gone as far as she could go and being busy with her own family, she passed the book along to me.

Beginning in 1996, I sent away for everything that was connected to my adoption. I registered with the Missouri Adoption Information Registry. I collected articles about reunions of children and their first families. Some of what came back was hopeful but most was discouraging.

One of the first documents I obtained was a copy of my adoption decree. All of the identifying information had been blacked out. The case number at the top matched with my non-identifying history. I received both documents from the Jackson County Juvenile Court. It was wonderful to read about my first mother and first father and their families. It provided me with a rough sketch where only shadows had been before.

My amended birth certificate was of little help. The hospital where I was born wasn't even mentioned.

My adoptive mother had told me I was adopted through Catholic Charities. In 1969 they operated the Florence Crittenton

Home for Unwed Mothers. To the right is copy of the letter I received from Florence Crittenton. It is like most of the other letters I got back. It told me that the facility I was inquiring about was no longer in possession of adoption files. They were turned over to the Jackson County Juvenile Court. The hospital, placement agency, law firm and maternity home were all banks, dead ends. I was constantly being detoured to the Jackson County Juvenile Court.

In March of 2003, I was hospitalized for kidney stones. After that very painful ordeal, my wife asked me if I had considered starting up my search again. Even though I had run into the same obstacles my sister had, I was ready to begin once more.

By the middle of July, I had sent out another series of request letters. Following the suggestion of the search book, I took a chance and sent a request to Jackson County asking for adoption agency records and hospital records. It got me nowhere. So I picked up the phone and called them.

I spoke with Rosalee Schottel, a Legal Assistant in the Family Court Division. I asked her why it was so difficult for me to find out information about my adoption. She told me that I was supposed to run into dead ends. That's the way the law is in Missouri, she explained.

I was told that everything related to my adoption, even the request letters I had sent to her office, was permanently closed in my adoption file. Ms. Schottel said there is nothing in the state that says I can gain access to anything in my adoption file.

She took me through each step of contacting my first parents as detailed in Missouri Law. I had her explain it to me a second time. Being a visually oriented person, I drew out a flow chart so that I would understand it better.

Sadly I informed her that I was not able to obtain consent from both of my adoptive parents. I went on to explain that the Florence Crittenton home was closed along with every other institution involved in my adoption. My road ended at her desktop.

With my option file open before her, Ms. Schottel told me that I wasn't born at the Crittenton home but at The Willows Hospital.

She went on to say, according to some accounts, if they are to be believed, that all of the records from the Willows were burned in a bonfire in the front yard.

SAY WHAT?

I found out where I was born but that news was soured by hearsay of torched records. I was stunned. Not only were my first parents a mystery but so was the place where I came into this world.

Back I went to my search file. My adoption decree had all of its identifying information blanked out except in the last paragraph. Right there, all along was the name of the adopted. Me. Jonathan.

Following the advice of my wife and focusing on one particular clue contained in my non-identifying social history, I was soon hot on the trail.

I made many phone calls to historical societies, chambers of commerce and libraries. Through old city directories, programs and obituaries, I learned the identity, phone number and current address of my first mother. I had a third party, Sarah, contact her.

At 5:30 that night, I got a call from Sarah. "I just can't," is what my first mother told Sarah in response to my request to make contact. My first mother told Sarah that she was a private person and wanted her privacy respected. Sarah told me that they talked for about a half hour. My first mother explained that no one in her life knows about me. She said that she thought about me often, especially on my birthday.

Sarah requested any new family medical history. My first mother said that she and her siblings were all healthy. Her mother has Alzheimers and her father died of kidney cancer some years before.

Ten minutes after they finished their conversation, my first mother called Sarah back. Again she said that she could not make contact.

I was so saddened by this rejection that I couldn't finish my conversation with Sarah. I handed the phone to my wife who ended the call.

Over the following weeks, I sought meaning and direction. The questions of my origins still lingered. I shared my discovery with my sister. The good and the bad of it. Together we prayed for comfort and guidance. Since I now knew that we were both adopted through the Willows, I sent her all of my information I had gathered on the place.

I sought perspective from other women who had similar experiences as my own first mother. It tore me up inside to think that my contacting her opened up a very old wound. Painful memories that she had to console by herself since nobody else knew her secret. I was unsure what my next step was.

I have not mentioned my first mother's name in my story out of respect for her privacy. Even my full name, given to me by my first mother, is partially obscured in the image on the web site.

I attempted to contact her a second time in late September. My letter came back with a note insisting on no further contact.

It took me almost seven years to locate my first mother. In that time I prepared myself for much of the mental and emotional anguish I encountered. Thankfully I have had the love and support of my wife and family. Though it saddens me greatly, I am prepared to meet my death without ever meeting the woman who gave me life. All my effort and good intentions cannot change what is in her heart.

Now, I am dedicated to solving the mysteries of the Willows Maternity Sanitarium. There was so much secrecy and shame that surrounded it's walls. A safe harbor to some. An empty hole in the ground to others. Shedding light on the truth and giving voice to the stories will begin the healing process for so many who lost a part of themselves there.

Scott Moore

Mary Etta, 1948 - I was born May 18, 1948 at The Willows. My adoptive parents had waited 13 years to have a baby and when they weren't able, they adopted me. I came with three pieces of information - my crib card with description of my birth parents, my birth mother's lab sheet showing she was infection free with a name on it and my footprints.

I began my search in February of 2003. Using my adoption paperwork, with my last name as a starting point, I applied for my non-identifying information. I got on the internet and started searching for my grandparents on genealogy sites. When I found a possible match, I contacted the person who submitted the information. He gave me more details and I called a possible sister of my birth mother. She confirmed that I was her sister's child and later called and gave me her phone number and address. When I called her, she said no, and hung up. I do have contact with the aunt and she has sent me family pictures. She told me that my birth mother has never told anyone that she had me.

The aunt gave me the nickname and last name of my birth father. Back to the genealogy sites, and I found my birth father. My birth parents had married, divorced and had another child who was killed. His name was on the site, listing both parents, which gave me my birth father's full name. I called one of his brothers to see where he lived and confirmed that I had the right one. I called him and he admitted he was my birth father, but said he was never sure I had been born.

I never lied when I called a possible family member. I told them I was doing genealogy research and asked some questions. I was lucky to find them and really lucky to be able to establish a relationship with someone in the birth family. I have the medical information that I need for my children, my grandchildren and myself.

I hope that each of you will have some success in your searches.
Mary Etta

Perry, 1939 - The search for my birthparents began relatively late in my life. After I retired from a career with the telephone company, I had time to do some of the things I always wanted to do but never seemed to have the time. But was I too late to start? I had known I was adopted from the time I was about 5 years old and had thought about it many times during my life but never wanted to look while my adoptive parents were alive. I had the same feelings many adoptees have, that my parents had done so much in giving me a wonderful life and I didn't want to "hurt" them by looking for my birthparents. They might take such a search as an indication of a lack of love for them. However, in mid 1995, when a good friend of mine was going to be visiting Kansas City, Missouri, I kidded about him going to city hall and finding out the "truth" about me. All I ever had in the past was an official paper saying that my birth certificate was on file in Jackson County Missouri. However, I did tell my friend to get any forms necessary to obtain a birth certificate. When he returned with the necessary forms I did look at them for several months before deciding to make the effort to see what I could find. I did send for and receive the certificate which was, of course, amended with adoptive parents' names, but it did give the attending physician's name and an address where I was born.

I didn't exactly know what to do with this information from this point and thought about hiring an investigator. However, in looking through the Cleveland classified phone directory I saw a listing for something called The Adoption Network of Cleveland. When I called and hesitantly told the person at the other end of the line that I was thinking of searching but was not sure what to do and if this organization might help, she replied "bingo." This was one of the most fortunate days of my life because a month later I was sitting in my first Adoption Network Cleveland meeting. For the first time in my life I was with others that were discussing some of the same feeling that I had always had, wondering what my roots were and why I was different from those who could talk about their ancestors. People who could understand why I sometimes would get angry when My adoptive parents would talk on and on about their relatives and I would envision a "black hole" prior to the day I was born. It was the first of many insightful meetings with a great support organization.

Through the Adoption Network Cleveland I was given names of people to contact in Kansas City to discuss some of my questions. Missouri is notorious for their strict closed adoption policies. When I told one of the contacts the address on my birth certificate, she replied, "That's the address of The Willows, a reputable maternity home that existed here in Kansas City from 1908 until 1969." What a revelation just knowing where I had come into the world. I followed up using legal means to get my non-identifying information and gave a court approved investigator a retainer to help in locating my birthmother. The information I received from the county had indicated that she was 27 at the time of my birth and had been educated through the eighth grade. All that the official investigator would say was that I had a very unusual last name that he could not divulge it to me unless he had approval from my birthparents (a legal requirement in Missouri). He had no luck getting more information and time was dragging on.

During this same time I was also getting involved with search postings on the internet through AOL. Through these contacts I got the name of a non-official investigator from some people I was e-mailing regarding my adoption situation. Discussions with The Adoption Network Cleveland confirmed that this person had a good reputation. After a payment of $250.00 I had my birth name within one week. It turned out that the name was unusual because there are only 15 or so listed on the internet for the entire United States. But where do I go from here? An online friend who knew what to do checked the Social Security Death Index and discovered a woman with the same last name who was 27 at the time of my birth. Unfortunately she had died in Connecticut in 1998. Could this woman from Connecticut have been my birthmother?

I finally had enough information to go to a search Workshop given by the Adoption Network Cleveland. It was there that I was advised to get a copy of this woman's obituary and send a short, non-threatening letter to some of her relations. The letter would tell them who I was and that I was looking for possible relatives. In September of 1997 I sent out 6 letters to 6 strangers in Connecticut and Massachusetts. Five days later I received a telephone call from one of them asking just who I was and that I had their family buzzing about these letters from Cleveland. He said the woman I was talking about was his aunt but that she was single all her life and as far as he knew, she never had any children. I sent copies of my non-identifying information showing him what led me to write to members of his family. Armed with this information he began questioning older members of his family. On October 4, 1997, a day I will always remember, I received an e-mail that began, "Perry, it looks like you have found your birthmother." I found out that my aunt was pregnant and was sent away to have a child. A secret of the family that had been brought out of the closet and into the light of day and most importantly, I had found my roots. Since that day in October I have worked with my birthmother's family and the Jackson County Family Court in Missouri to receive my official records. Two days before Christmas in 1997 I opened a document that positively linked me to the woman I found in Connecticut.

My birthmother's family has been very open and gracious about telling me about my birthmother and how much she was loved by all the family. I now have many pictures of her as well as pictures of her parents, sisters, brothers, nephews and nieces. Unfortunately many of those close relatives have passed away. I was invited to a family reunion in Connecticut in June of 1998 and met all of my new relatives. I was even able to place some flowers on her grave. Since then we have kept up a cordial correspondence by letters and e-mails.

Although I began my search rather late in life and my birthmother has passed away, I've had a lot of questions I've had buried deep inside me for a long time answered. I found out that it is never too late and I owe a debt of gratitude to the Adoption Network Cleveland and all the others who helped me find the woman who gave me life.

Perry

Sue, 1948 - I was born at The Willows May 3, 1948. My adoption papers said I was named Annabel Stroup and my mom's name was Gloria. I have searched for many years and haven't been able to locate my birth mom. My adoptive parents were great but have died and I have no family left. Would love to know more.

Sue Kummer

Russell, 1965 - To whom it may concern, I was born at the Willows and would like as much info on the place that you have. I am interested in corresponding with anyone else who was born at the Willows or any first mothers who might like to talk about it, especially if they were there in the 60's. I will look forward to hearing from you.

Russell Mettlach

Tommy, 1965 - I have known for as long as I can remember that I was adopted but I was told that I was not to talk about it at a very young age, so I kept inside of me a secret that I could not share with anyone.

The agency did a remarkable job placing me and it was a tall order. I'm bi-racial and in 1965 that had to be tough. I can easily be mistaken for white and most people are surprised to find out that I consider myself to be African-American.

When I was young I would sit out on the front porch and imagine that my mother, my first mother was somewhere thinking about me. Thunderstorms always trigger this longing, maybe it means something, maybe it doesn't.

So all my life I played the game until last year in a period of extreme depression, I just couldn't play anymore. I then learned that my sister was adopted too. She had asked my father before his death about being adopted and he denied it although his brother filled us in on all the details he knew.

So to that my nasty secret was out of the closet. I decided that maybe I should try and find my mom. Thank God for the internet. The only clue I had was the name of the doctor on my birth certificate, R.A. Slickman. I figured that they wouldn't have had any reason to change that and I was right. An interesting side note, when I was a youngster Dr. Slickman was still listed in the phone book and I almost called him. But I figured he wouldn't help me so I chickened out.

Little did I know that his name would start me down a road that would bring me closer than ever to finding my mother. I entered his name in Google and discovered he was a staff doctor at a maternity home called The Willows.

I was on the right trail. I found a lot of information on The Willows including a message board where I discovered that I could request my non-identifying information and that's what I did. Keep in mind at this time in my life, 37 years old, I didn't have a clue even what race I was, what city I was born in, nothing.

The day finally arrived for me to pick up my white-out redacted copies and my whole image of ME changed. I discovered I was mixed race (a surprise to the dear lady at records department who thought they had made a mistake placing me with a black family).

My mother was a 19 year old young lady of German heritage from a broken home that lived with her mother and step-father. She was described as artistic (that's where my daughter gets her talent). Ironic that I was stationed in Germany for a number of years in the Army and I felt and looked as if I had a home, my daughter was even born in Germany. We use to tease her and tell her she was really a German; little did I know how close to home that hit.

My dad was a 27 year old black man who worked for a vet. They met because of a sick cat that she found in her back yard. He helped her with the cat and a little more I dare say. At first they considered marriage but the reality of inter-racial marriage in the 60's set in and instead they broke up.

She was about to move in with a friend when her dad showed up and talked her into going to the Willows to have me. The rest is history.

I would love to meet my parents, my adopted ones have now both passed away and I feel a little lonely. I plan on doing a reunion search but I worry that my mom won't want to let a secret like me out.

I don't know maybe when it's raining and the thunder is rolling, she really is thinking about me. I hope so.

That's my story about The Willows. It made me feel better to write this down. Who knows, maybe my mom will read this and reach out to me. She has some really wonderful grandchildren that I think anyone would be proud of and I didn't turn out too shabby either. Thanks for your web site. It has been a pleasure sharing my story with you.

Thomas A. Diggs

1947 - Deborah Baker O'Connor was born April 17, 1947 at The Willows. She lost her battle with Leukemia January 25, 2000. A bone marrow transplant from her birth family may have saved her life.

Because of Missouri's sealed original birth certificates, Debby never even knew their names.

1999 - After locating her mother through a registry which locates people throughout the United States, Janice was able to contact her birth mother for the first time. Her mother, Sally, lives in Milwaukee, Wis. Janice said finding Sally was her personal miracle from God. Only one week after signing up on the registry, she was able to locate her mother. Sally had been on the registry for 12 years.

Janice, 40, came into this world with the name Faith W. She said she had a wonderful childhood and two loving parents but always felt like she was missing something in her life. After many years of praying for a miracle which would reunite Janice with her birth mother, her prayers were answered.

She was able to contact an adoption investigator through the internet to find out some information she needed to locate her birth mother. She knew she was born in Kansas City, MO., at Willows Hospital on July 4, 1958. Her mother was scared and unmarried.

By going online she was able to find out that Sally, who was 16 at the time, lived in the hospital for the last few months of her pregnancy and then went back to her home town. She was able to rock baby Faith for 30 minutes before turning her over to a new family. Sally told her daughter that she carried an image of her child burned in her mind with her through the years.

She said, "The very first thing I want you to know is that there was never a day that went by in my life that I didn't think about you," Janice said. "She told me I have my father's eyes and that I'm left-handed like my father was."

Her biological father died when she was 10 years old. She said she wished she could also have met him.

FROM BEDGIE.TRIPOD.COM

FROM BEDGIE.TRIPOD.COM
2008 - 2010 Guestbook

From B. Roller - My husband and I adopted two boys that were born at The Willows. The first one was born 8-15-62 with the name Kevin. He was very ill for a time after his birth and was under a doctor's care until they felt he was able to be dismissed from the home. The second one was born 3-2-65 and was William while at the Willows. They were both 2 and 3 months old when we were proudly able to bring them into our home. We have been blessed so much to have them all these years…a long with their little sister who was born 6-27-70 and was adopted through another agency. I would very much like to meet the mothers of these two boys and thank them for their brave decision to give us our boys. If there are any other adoptees or mothers who were in The Willows about the times of our boys birth, I would very much like to hear from you. Thanks so much for this site…..good luck to you all. God Bless you greatly.

From Kay T - I am a Willows birth mom of April 1, 1958, baby girl Rody. A rude awakening for me, the father refused and after birth we tried to get baby girl Rody back and were rejected. We married with 4 more children. She eventually found us and to date, she is happily reunited with her birth dad, my husband and not with me. I can never accept nor handle this and I am deeply depressed since March 1998. Be careful all of you out there. I would love to share memories with those there at my time. I was known as Jeanie Woods. WHAT A NEW WORLD OF CHANGE.

From Kathy D - My first entry was 3-18-05 and I was looking for my son born 6-28-66. I found him 1-28-07. April of last year I drove to Wichita, KA to meet him and his family. When I saw him, it was like looking back at myself. We are so very much alike. Not just features but the way we talk, hold our heads, react with other people and write. Both of us have been school teachers, he is now a principal of a high school. His wife is wonderful and his 2 children are out of this world. I have just had my prayers answered. He had a great family growing up and I just love him, plain and simple. I would give my life for him and my grandchildren. There is plenty of love to go around. If you are looking, keep going. I found the right person who had the info. In less than a day I had the name and address of my son. Within hours we were talking and haven't stopped. We are like a pair of old shoes now, comfortable.

My name is Nancy (Hale) Good. I'm searching for my son, birth name Kevin Hale, born September 5, 1961 at The Willows, Kansas City, MO. I keep running into walls no matter who I contact. I have registered my search information with the Johnson County Courts. They tell me nothing can be done unless the adoptee and the adoptive parents request the records opened in order to contact me. At that point they can match his birth records to my registered request. I don't mean to interfere with his life. I only want to answer any questions he may have and provide him with health history. Giving your child up is something you never get over or forgive yourself for, the love and ache never go away. Thanks for the chance to at least put this in writing.

From James Lee S. - I was born on May 10, 1945 at The Willows and was named Archer Alexander. My mother's name was Phyllis Alexander and she was from the Cessna Park area, in Illinois. Her mother's name was Rosa. There was no information about who my father was. My mother had four pictures of one man, nobody can identify, in her photo album. She was with him around the time I was conceived. He could be my father. M. J. Kessler, Y 3/C, USNR, Maritime Unit, San Clemente, California was his address at one time. In one of the pictures he was with a friend, Charles Petersen, SC 2/C (Ship's Cook, Second Class). If you think you know either of these men, I will furnish a photograph. M. J. Kessler should have been in Washington DC. In August of 1944. Still searching.

Michael W - I was born at The Willows on May 24, 1951 and have some records. My birth mother was from a wealthy family in Palisades, CA. I was adopted to a family in Central Missouri and have a copy of those adoption records. I do have a copy of a picture taken of me at the age of 3 weeks at The Willows. I have been lucky enough to find out who my birth parents are and have met them in the last 5 years. The state of Missouri still refuses to give me a copy of my original birth certificates.

Marilyn M - I had baby girl Roxanne 4-19-52. Still looking for her. I was an unwed mother forced by her mother to give up my daughter. I really wanted to keep her. I was a maid at The Willows during my tenure there. I slept in the basement and tended to other pregnant girls. We weren't supposed to hold our baby but I would sneak in every chance I could to hold Roxanne and kiss her.

Beulah S - I gave birth to a baby girl on Jan. 24, 1958 at The Willows in K.C. Mo. They told me she was stillborn but I heard her cry, however when I asked to see her they said I could not. I would love to know the truth about her birth. I named her Bobbi Leah. I have never believed that she was stillborn but cannot prove it.

Jeanne S B - I am a 2949 graduate of The Willows and connected with maternal birth family in 2001 but the paternal side declined acknowledgement so I have very little knowledge on that side and, of course, due to the archaic Missouri adoption laws, no original birth certificate. May we all find peace in knowing that we were loved by our birth mothers very much. I also signed earlier today but reading more postings I would like to inform all of you that by calling or writing to the Circuit Court of Jackson County, Missouri, Family Court Division, 625 East 26th Street, Kansas City, MO, 64108 (816)435-4788, you can find out the procedure for obtaining identifying and/or non identifying information on your Willows graduate (adoptee) and that The International Soundex Registry is a great organization for help. Google it. Good luck to everyone searching for a child or a parent. I would like to hear the experience of a woman who gave birth at The Willows. My birth mother passed in 1996 and I did not find her/her family until 2000 so I don't know that side of the story - did our moms name us, did they see us, hold us or anything like that? Just some questions. Peace.

FROM CHILDREN OF ADOPTEES

FROM CHILDREN OF ADOPTEES

FROM QUILTED HISTORY - 2005 (On the internet)

In some cases the people originally involved in the triad are deceased incapacitated or have simply given up the search. Their children sometimes take up the torch. It's harder for them to find information because in most cases it is only released to the parties directly involved. Still they remain optimistic.

I began this Willows Maternity Sanitarium webpage sometime around March 1998. This page was my personal plea for information regarding The Willows Maternity Sanitarium, which was somewhat nonexistent on the internet at that time. This was also my way of getting information out there about my grandmother, who was born December 15, 1924 at The Willows, and named Martha Seberger.

Within two weeks of her birth, Martha Seberger was adopted by Gus and Jennie Maier, who changed Martha's name to Betty

Jane Meier. Betty had two older brothers and one younger brother, all biological children of Gus and Jennie. Then Jennie gave birth to a daughter and Betty's life changed. Although Gus continued to dote on his adoptive daughter, mother Jennie soon began to treat Betty as "Cinderella." Betty never understood the change in her mother, until by accident, she learned she had been adopted.

Betty grew up and found the love of her life. They married and had four children of their own. Through all of this, Betty felt a curiosity about her biological parents. In the 1950's Betty wrote to The Willows. She described her tumultuous childhood and longing to find her birth parents. To paraphrase, The Willows wrote in response that she should forget about the past, now that she is married and has children, and should "just move on with her life." Betty's young son, who would become my father, promised his mother that he would someday help her find her parents.

My grandparents struggled financially throughout their marriage. But in early 1968, they decided they were going to take their first "real" vacation, a trip to Florida. Betty had suffered with ulcers and had decided to have an operation before the trip. Shortly after surgery, while in the recovery room, Betty complained of a headache, then immediately passed away. Prior to surgery, (I'm told this was normal procedure at the time), a block was placed under her neck then her head strapped down. Her head had been strapped down too tightly, a clot had formed, and when the strap and block were removed, the clot made its way to her brain. She was only 43 years old.

Through the years, my father never forgot the promise he made to his mother. At some point, he wrote to Missouri and received non-identifying information, we learned that my grandmother had been born Martha Seberger. A copy of an infant medical test showed that her birth mother was "Mayme Seberger." We assumed that this was an alias created by the birth mother or The Willows to shield the birth mother's identity. Eventually, we came to believe that perhaps Seberger was my grandmother's legal birth surname. We had seen the name Seberger on a few other papers and concluded that any legal documents probably had to be signed with the birth mother's legal last name.

I shared my grandmother's story with an adoption ANGEL. Through various contacts, she discovered that my grandmother's birth certificate might not be sealed. It might be one that fell through the legal cracks. My hopes soared! Would I finally discover "birthmother Seberger's" real first name? I immediately found the necessary paperwork to request the birth certificate. I never mentioned anything about adoption or adopted. Within a week I received a response stating that, although they had my grandmother's name, date and place of birth, they needed her parent's names. Grrr! I thought I was sunk. Instead of writing back, I phoned and explained that my grandmother passed away when I was one year old (true), she did not know her father's name because he did not raise her (true), and that I knew her mother's maiden name was Seberger. I hear the woman punching in a few things on the computer, then she said, "Here it is. Since we've already received your payment, I'll have this sent out to you right away." My heart was racing but I still couldn't let myself believe.

And isn't it ironic, at various points in my childhood, my family lived within 20 miles of Mayme Seberger, who passed away in 2000 at the age of 97. Mayme never had any more biological children.

Who could have imagined that the birth certificate had not been sealed? If only we had known, which is why I share this story. No matter what you are told, try anyway. Don't mention "red-flag" words like adoption, adopted, amended, maternity home, original, birth parents and adoptive parents.

Alma "Ruth", 1935 - I ran across your web site today, 12 Nov. 2003, and found it to be very interesting. I do have an old pamphlet from The Willows, not sure from what year. I am guessing the late 30's.

Several years ago I searched very hard for a child my grandmother had given birth to while staying at The Willows. The only information that I have is that the baby was born to my grandmother Alma "Ruth" Eldred on or close to May 6, 1935. The baby was a female with dark hair and blue eyes. My grandmother at the time was 15. The father of the child was Oscar Potter and he was 24 or 25 at the time. The baby was adopted by an older couple from the Tulsa, OK. area.

Tracy Vandegrift

Ardus, 1920 - I was overjoyed to find this web site about the Willows. My mother is Jessie Elaine Heller, born Oct. 12, 1920 at The Willows. Her name at birth was Ardus Graning. She was adopted by William Adolph Heller and Maggie Rebekah Sherman Heller. She is currently 83 years old and living in Windsor, CO.

I have a copy of my mother's adoption decree from the Circuit Court of Jackson County. We are currently trying to get a copy of her original and altered birth certificate. If you can give me any information, I would be greatly appreciative.

Thank you,

Ardus Suzanne Whatley

Dale, 1926 - My father was born at the Willows May 3, 1926. The description of the first parents read that the mother was 19 years old, 5 Ft. 2 1/2 inches and had reddish brown hair with brown eyes. Weight was 124 lbs. She was in the last year of high with four years of piano, six months of vocal, student, town reared and an American. The father was described as being 24 years old, 5 Ft. 8 inches with brown hair and blue eyes and 145 lbs. He was a farmer, country reared, some high school and an American.

The doctor's name was Dr. J. W. Kepner. My father was named baby Dale. Four months later he was adopted for the full price of $26.00 by August and Minnie Kloepper who lived in Baileyville,

Kansas. What I've read about babies being adopted out is that they try to match the babies to parents according to looks, hair color, bone structure, nationality, etc.

Grandpa was a large German man with red hair. Grandma was a very large bone structure woman with a weight problem with dark hair. My father was a fairly small man with a fiery temper, olive complexion and dark black hair with brown eyes. He used to tell me when I was a child that he was Indian. I wonder if he was really an Italian.

Grandma and Grandpa named the baby Carl Dale Kloepper. There was an adoption number of 4850. Grandpa talked at times that he knew the last name of the parents or one of the parents and that name is Bell. He also told a story about how he went to the father at one time when Dale was sick to get some financial help. Dales' birth father worked at a gas station according to my Grandpa.

My father had heard a story that his birth mother went up north to break into show business. It is unknown whether this is actual truth or a fable. No birth certificate is on file or if it was at the time of his retirement it was sealed.

My daughter and I gave up for a few years but his birth origin was always on our minds especially when medical problems had arisen in our family. I even had someone check into this and all the person said was that there were no records found. The woman also explained that it was common for a child to be born out of wedlock in those days in Kansas. It was a wild town. I think she got tired of looking and I can't blame her.

Jeannie

George, 1943 - My father was born at The Willows hospital July 15, 1943. His birth mother named him George Nelson. He was a healthy baby and was adopted by James and Maurine Lacy, both of Kansas City, through the Cradle. The adoption was finalized in 1944.

He was told that his birth mother was from the Northwest part of Missouri around Platte or Buchanan Counties. She was said to be in her early 30's and from a farming family …a large farm. I know nothing about the birth father.

George/David was very Irish looking. He had very rosy cheeks and when he was flush from exercise or was embarrassed they would get very red. He was 6 ft. 1 inch with long legs and very thin through most of his life. He had medium brown hair and blue/green eyes that would turn dark green when angry. His beard was red when he grew it long. His toes were especially long and I have the same large feet and toes. When nervous he would stick out his tongue without realizing it or chew on his tongue. He liked to rock himself to sleep at night while moving his leg.

He had a drinking problem, was easily angered and was always feeling anxious. He was in the Navy from 1961 to 1966. The genetics must be very strong as my brother is exactly like him in looks, mannerisms, thought process.

His adopted parents were very wealthy people and could afford to adopt and raise a child in the best of circumstances. They had lost a son to crib death in 1942 and spotted Dave in 1943. He was an adorable baby and toddler with pudgy cheeks and a smile that could melt a mother.

He was diagnosed with high blood pressure in his 40s and diabetes in his 50s. He passed away unexpectedly this year, 2003, of a massive heart attack. He had no knowledge of any heart problems. The doctors, in trying to save him, found his coronary arteries over 90% blocked. We really need medical history on him for my children, my brother's children and for us.

He married 3 times but only had my brother from his first marriage. He abandoned us and we had a difficult time getting close to him most of his life. Thankfully, in the last 5 years of his life, I believe we did.

He had his appendix taken out at 7. Other than that he was very healthy child.

I would love to hear about any information that is out there. Mother, father, siblings, uncles, aunts, cousins - any information.

Barbara Lacy

Natalie, 1953 - My grandmother had a baby boy at The Willows January 20, 1953. Here is every detail and piece of information I know to be true as per conversations with my grandmother before she passed away November 2002.

Her name was Natalie Juedeman. She was a single mother of two other children: daughter, Lynn who was my mother and a son, Lee from a previous marriage. She was dating a man and became pregnant. When she notified the birth father of her pregnancy, he informed her he could and would do nothing for her and the baby. He was married and had a family. This came as a surprise to her.

Because she was a single mother with two children already, Natalie decided to give this third baby up for adoption. She planned on transporting herself and her children to Texas to have the child. This would eliminate the stigma of being pregnant out of wedlock amongst her friends and family. Eventually she was convinced by her father to stay in Kansas City and have the child at The Willows. Natalie's father was a Kansas City, Missouri police officer and knew the reputations of the maternity homes in the city. Arrangements were made with other family members to take care of her daughter and son. The rest of the family was given the cover story that she was out of town on a job.

She checked into the home about 4-5 months before the baby was due. She used her real name while in the home and that name was also used on the child's birth certificate. Natalie's stay at The Willows occurred during the Christmas holiday. Her father helped her sneak out in the middle of the night to spend time with her family on Christmas Eve. After opening presents with her children, she was taken back to The Willows before daylight on Christmas morning.

She had a baby boy and was named Ronald Lee Juedeman after his birth-brother. She gave him the same name because she knew she would occasionally call out or talk in her sleep. If she did call out his name, whoever would hear her would think she was calling out her son's name.

She said she was neither able to nor chose to hold him after he was born. She did see him after delivery and once more before she left the home. The Willows handled the delivery and the adoption. She was white, Christian and of Jewish decent but doubted that that information was on the birth certificate. Her age at time of birth was 26. She was single/divorced. Her father's name was William Max Finke and mother's name was Mabel Verna Finke. Her home address at the time was 4043 Bales, Kansas City, Missouri. Her place of birth was Kansas City, Missouri. This was her third and final child and pregnancy.

My grandmother did not want to intrude on her son's life. She said that if he had found her, she would welcome him into her life with open arms and an open heart. My mother and uncle wanted to find him before she died but her intentions on continued searches were made very clear. She wanted all attempts to find him to stop until she had passed away. After a lengthy battle with lung cancer, she died in November of 2002.

I'd like my grandmother's son to know that he has a half sister and half brother as well as nieces and nephews that would like to find him. We all would welcome him into our families. My mother and uncle can not register with the Missouri Adoption Information Registry because they are half siblings. I have filled out a form with the International Soundex Reunion Registry and posted the adoptee birth facts on many web sites and in many newsletters. I can't think of anything else to do.

Debby

Phillip Willm, 1947 - I am searching for any information surrounding the birth of my father who was born at the Willows. His adopted name was Gaylord Lynn Wright and his parents were Floyd E. and Norma H. Wright. He was fatally injured in a farm accident when I was 4 years old. His adoptive parents were the best parents to him and grandparents to me and my brother. They loved us with fierce and unconditional love that made me what I am today. They did not adopt any other children, as my dad had a problem with his hips that required medical treatment. They felt they should give him their total attention in order to deal with his medical trouble.

My grandparents are both deceased. My grandmother just passed away in August at the age of 94 so I am just getting started with my search for dad's first parents. I did not want her to think that she was inferior in any way so I did not want to search until she had passed. My mother has nothing to do with me and my brother is also deceased. I am feeling a need to find a biological connection to my dad. Also I would like any medical information for myself and my 3 sons.

My father was born at the Willows Maternity Sanitarium on August 10, 1947 at 11:30 a.m. He weighed 7 pounds 10 ounces and was 20 inches long with a 13 1/2inch head and 14 inch chest. He was named Phillip Willm. I also have a lab report from the Sackett Laboratory on 4-19-1947 by a Dr. D.T. Van Del for a patient named Patricia. The report states that BLOOD: Kahn negative; Smear for gonococci negative.

I have some information regarding his first parents. His first mother was 19 at the time of his birth, weighing 120 pounds and was 5 ft. 2 inches with light brown hair and brown eyes. She was a high school grad with 6 years of piano study. His first father was 18 at the time of birth, weighing 170 pounds and was 5 ft. 6 inches with blond hair and blue eyes. He was a high school grad and an excellent figure skater. He was Catholic with German extractions. I can get no information from Missouri as both my dad and his parents are deceased.

I have been able to get some information from Kansas as that is where they lived. I know that his first mother's date of birth is March 19, 1928. Her reason for giving him up for adoption was because she was not ready to assume responsibility for a child. She was working as a distribution clerk for an electric company at the time she became pregnant. I also found out that his first father wanted to marry her but her family was opposed to that. This could be because she was Methodist and he Catholic. Maybe they ended up getting married after all.

My grandmother was great about keeping all his important adoption papers together and safe. I have the court paper from the Circuit Court of Jackson County, Missouri at Kansas City. It is number A.16067. It also lists the guardian ad item as Richard B. Birwan. It also states that the complete decree of adoption of Phillip Willm papers in the Adoption Record in book no 13 at page no. 234. His amended birth certificate is under the file number of 54675-47.

It is my understanding from the news story from this website that the girls were given names when they entered the Willows so Patricia may or may not be any help. I also do not know if Willm is also an alias. Since I cannot access any information from Missouri I am at a loss of where to go from here. Thank you for this website. It is very good. I like reading about The Willows as it makes me feel closer to my dad. I have registered with ISSR and posted information on the beige website for the Willows.

Lori Wright Janice

Vance, 1926. My name is Steven Sellers and I am looking for information about my father's biological parents. He was born in The Willows Maternity Sanitarium on April 28, 1926. His given name at birth was Vance and we believe, although I have no verification, that his last name was Wilson or Willson. He was adopted by Ralph and Isabella Sellers.

Dad's natural birth father was twenty-one, 6 feet tall and 165 pounds with brown hair and blue eyes. He had a high school education and was employed as a shipping clerk but I don't know where. His mother was eighteen, 5'7" and 135 pounds. That's all the information I have.

Dad died at the age of 66 on December 16, 1992 of congestive heart failure. For most of his life he had no desire to learn anything about his parents but eventually decided to find out what he could but by then, he was told that all records from The Willows had been destroyed (editor's note: There's no definitive proof about the existence or destruction of Willows Hospital records).

My mom tried to get information from the state of Missouri but didn't have much luck.

I have one sister and two daughters so the "family name" doesn't extend very far. Along with the help of a friend who is gathering information through Ancestry.com, I am trying to find out as much as I can about my dad's family.

If anyone has any information I would really appreciate hearing from you. If you have any suggestions about what other options may be available, I would be happy to hear what they may be. Thanks for listening and sharing!

Steven V. Sellers

Virginia, 1915 - My mother was born at The Willows May 8, 1915. She had told me that her given name was Virginia White, however after reading everything that others have posted, it seems that no one had a last name when born. I know she found out her name when my grandfather died in 1965. She was adopted by Joseph LeCuyer and Ella Thorpe-LeCuyer from Kankakee, Illinois. I always thought it was a coincidence that my grandfather was a conductor on the Illinois Central Train that ran between Chicago and Kansas City and my mother just so happened to be born in Kansas City. I thought maybe he could have been her birth father. The family never talked much about my mother's adoption. I also always wondered if her birth mother could have been related to the Thorpe's or LeCuyer's. My mom has passed away but since I look like she did, I always have wondered who she and I looked like. This is all the information I have but with the find of this website and the other I am finding so much about the hospital. Thanks. Good luck to all.

Debbie Falkenhan

William, 1936 -

I am the daughter of baby boy William born in 1936 before June. My dad sent many times for info only to keep getting nothing. He gave up; I can't though. My dad deserves better and I love him. The greatest gift would be just to know. We have all info The Willows sent to his adopted family. Letter and parentage was test court doc. We do not even know if birth mother told truth. Could be from mars. LOL anyway if anyone wants to help me with a miracle please let me know.

FROM PRISCILLA

FROM PRISCILLA

In 1919 a young couple named Roy and Stella Crist were married. A humble farm couple with very modest financial means, they had four babies over the course of six years. All these little ones died due to a congenital condition. Some lived a few days or weeks; one little boy lived six months. Roy and Stella longed to adopt a child and heard of an adoption agency called "The Willows," in Kansas City, Missouri. They applied to be an adoptive couple and were accepted. Invited to choose from several babies available for adoption, they chose a 10-day-old baby girl. The year was 1926. The adoption fee was $28. That child was my mother Neva.

The Willows adoption sanitarium was founded in 1905 by Cora and Edwin Haworth, an affluent couple who lived in the heart of Kansas City, Missouri in a beautiful, grand home. They had a heart for unwed mothers and wanted to create a safe haven, a place where young women could have complete anonymity, give birth to their babies and then go back to their homes to live out their lives without the scrutiny and judgment that was so common in those days. Most came to The Willows very early in their pregnancy and lived there until their baby was born.

Eventually The Willows grew to be one of the most respected and sought after adoption agencies in the US.

From 1905 to the early 1960s, over 35,000 babies were adopted from the Willows. They eventually opened a nursing school on the property and trained many nurses throughout their tenure as an adoption sanitarium.

Over the years, as I've heard the story of my grandparents Roy and Stella, and even see the tombstones of their four precious babies, I've often marveled~~how could a couple continue to hope for a child after so many catastrophic losses??

How were they not consumed with bitterness or anger? How did they keep their abiding and deep faith that God is good and loving and continue to trust Him with their hopes and dreams for a child to raise as their own?

Well, they did. I really don't know how they did. I guess it was due to God's grace.

And they adopted my mother Neva, who was the light of their lives. 😊:-)

On mother's 65th birthday 25 years ago, she and I had lunch. She said, "Priscilla, 65 years ago today, my biological mother had the courage to give me up for adoption to the most wonderful parents! How brave she was to do that. I am so thankful." I realized that day that if even ONE of Roy and Stella's babies had lived, my mother would have been adopted by another family...... .and I and nearly fifty other people would not have been born. The thought was staggering to me, and still is.

Early in our marriage Jeff and I had dinner with his grandparents on his mother's side. As I looked through his grandmother's scrapbook, I saw a picture of The Willows. I said, "Why, grandmother, that's where my mother was born!" She replied, "Well honey, The Willows was started by my parents, Cora and

Edwin. That little girl in the picture is me. I sometimes was allowed to take care of the babies. I probably bathed your mama when she was born!"

All my life I'd heard about The Willows from my mother. Until that day I was unaware that Jeff's great-grandparents founded and ran this amazing home for unwed mothers. That Cora was the "kind matron of the home" grandmother Stella wrote about in her beautiful baby book. The book in which she described the supremely joyful day they picked up their new baby girl that they were blessed to raise to adulthood. :-)

So now, you know the REST of the story.

The Lord TRULY does work in mysterious ways!

MISCELLANEOUS

MISCELLANEOUS

In sixty-four years it was thought that from 25,000 to 35,000 babies were born at The Willows. The Willows had a basement full of birth records that no local bureau of vital statistics would accept for inclusion in their files.

I found a few fees mentioned that may be of interest. In 1936 prospective adoptive parents would send a $5.00 fee with proper identification and referrals. Once the home was approved, the parents had a year to select a baby. The total adoption charge was $40.00, including the deposit, paid at the time the baby was taken home. The parents had to bring baby bottles with nipples, baby clothes and a name for the baby.

In 1902, three years before The Willows was founded, life expectancy was forty-seven in the United States; only 14 percent of homes had a bath tub; only 8 percent had a telephone; there were only 8,000 cars in the United States. And only 144 miles of paved roads.

The average wage was 22 cents an hour; the average worker made between $200 and $400 a year; more than 95 percent of all births took place in the home.

Ninety percent of all physicians had no college education. Instead, they attended medical schools many of which were condemned in the press and by the government as substandard.

In 1935 the average income was $1600 per year. The average rent was $22.00 per month. A new house cost $3,400.00. A new car was $625.00. A United States postage stamp was three cents.

Mrs. Maudene Lowe worked there fifty-three years on the hospital administration staff.

Mrs. Alice Dysart worked thirty years as superintendent of nurses.

Mrs. Nelle McKwen worked forty-eight years as head of adoption.

An advertisement for The Willows Maternity Home in the Kansas City Journal, Sunday, April 14, 1907:

An elegantly located commodiously roomed and neatly furnished and equipped home, offering unfortunate girls the comforts and pleasures of home life, with the added facilities of hospital equipment and services and perfect seclusion.

The Willows is located in a quiet, retiring residence neighborhood. It enjoys the patronage of the best class of patrons and physicians and has the endorsement of everyone acquainted with its work.

Light, airy, comfortable rooms; recently furnished and equipped throughout; some new features just now being added, including parlor and reading room exclusively for the use of patients; strictly modern in all home appointments including light, heat, hot and cold bath; two bath rooms; good table board; pleasing and agreeable associated and surroundings; piano, literature, games of amusement; capable and experienced nurses; reliable physician in attendance or patient may furnish her own physician if preferred; well appointed nursery for the care of the babies, until good homes are found for them. If adoption is desired; adoptions and baby wardrobe furnished without charge to patient; all correspondence confidential, in plain envelope; accommodations and charges adjusted to the patients requirements; reliable services and modest prices; out-of-town patients met at train.

For further information call, address or telephone confidentially, The Willows.

A newspaper article from 1909 called The Willows a high-society home for unwed pregnant women and an adoption agency for their babies. One woman born at The Willows told The Star in 1975 when she was here to challenge Missouri's courts to release the home's sealed adoption records, "Let's get this straight that it was no baby mill. They were fine upstanding people who ran the home and only the most socially prominent were taken in. It had a lot of snob appeal. The Willows was like the Ritz or the Waldorf of homes for unwed mothers. It cost more to go there than it did to attend a finishing school....The young women were recommended by prominent doctors throughout the United States."

1925 employees were as follows: Superintendent, 2 assistant superintendents, manager, assistant manager, bookkeeper and cashier, secretary, telephone operator and typist, 3 stenographers, advertising room girl, pediatrician, obstetrician, pathologist, superintendent of nurses, nursery supervisor, 20 student nurses, matron of nurses' home, housekeeper, cook, 6 kitchen and dining room girls, linen maid, floor maid, 6 laundry helpers, engineer, night fireman, maintenance man, 2 porters.

The fee for a four month stay in a private room at The Willows in 1962 was about $1,600.00 including medical bills for a normal delivery.

1920 STATISTICS

1920 STATISTICS

DISTRIBUTION BY STATES

Iowa	60
Missouri	56
Illinois	45
Oklahoma	44
Nebraska	30
South Dakota	16
Texas	11
Minnesota	10
Colorado	8
New Mexico	4
Indiana	4
Arkansas	3
Ohio	3
Tennessee	2

Alabama, New Jersey, Wisconsin, North Dakota, Connecticut, Pennsylvania, New York, California, Louisiana, Michigan, West Virginia each 1

OCCUPATION	
Home girls	134
School girls	68
Commercial	35
School teachers	22
Domestic	20
Clerical	19
Telephone operators	11
Dressmakers	9
Waitresses	9
Music teachers	5
Nurses	5
Factory	3
Graduate nurses	2
Milliners	1
Librarian	1
Assistant photographer	1
Unknown	12

EDUCATION	
Common school	122
One year high school	50
Two years high school	79
High school graduate	62
Commercial college	27
College	24
College graduate	2

AGE	
13 years old	1
14 years old	2
15 years old	11
16 years old	24
17 years old	43

18 years old	35
19 years old	48
20 years old	38
21 years old	25
22 years old	27
23 years old	26
24 years old	15
25 years old	10
26 years old	10
Over 26 years old	33
Average age	20

RELIGION	
Methodist	103
Baptist	47
Christian	42
Presbyterian	38
Lutheran	26
Catholic	26
Congregational	13
Episcopal	8
Evangelical	6
United Brethren	3
Church of Christ	3
Friends	2
Reformed	2
Jewish	1
Swedish Mission	1
Christian Science	1
Non-church member	13
Unknown	22

BIBLIOGRAPHY

BIBLIOGRAPHY
JACKSON COUNTY HISTORICAL SOCIETY
KANSAS CITY MISSOURI LIBRARY ARCHIVES
NEWSPAPER ARTICLES
BOOKS WRITTEN BY EDWIN PEARL HAWORTH
LETTERS FROM AN OLD WEBSITE, WILLOWS.ORG
RESEARCH PAPER OF JUNE 25, 2014 BY PAM MCPHEETERS
A WEBSITE FOUND BY BETHANY BOYD ABOUT PAWNEE BILL
FAMILY PHOTOGRAPH ALBUMS
FAMILY HISTORY
Bedgie.tripod.com

BOOKS
VINTAGE KANSAS CITY STORIES
PARIS OF THE PLAINS
EVERYDAY LIFE IN THE 1800s
TURNING LIFE INTO FICTION
DISCOVERING YOUR FEMALE ANCESTORS
THE WOMAN YOU WANT TO BE 1928 - 1942

OTHER BOOKS BY BEV VAN HORN

OTHER BOOKS BY BEV VAN HORN

Audio books of pioneer women's diaries:

Living Voices of the Past Series 1995 to 2000:

Covered Wagon Women: Diaries and Letters from the Western Trails, 1850, by Margaret A. Frink

Covered Wagon Women: Diaries and Letters from the Western Trails, 1851, by Lucia Williams

Vanished Arizona by Martha Summerhayes

Desert Wife by Hilda Faunce

Print Books:

Early History of Mineral and Rio Grande Counties, Colorado 1880 to 1980, in 2000.

Best Friends Are Like Suspenders: They Hold You Up When You Are Falling Down, 2004.

Civil War Record of D. M. Haworth - my great-grandfather's diary of his Civil War days.

Bev worked for the Independence Daily Reporter while in high school as a proof reader and society editor.

Bev Van Horn was a journalism major at Christian College, Columbia, Missouri and Kansas University.

She was in advertising for The Lawrence Outlook weekly newspaper in Lawrence, Kansas 1965.

She was a reporter for the Gardner News, Gardner, Kansas 1968-1973

She was editor of the Summit Sentinel in Summit County, Colorado 1973 - 1975.

She co-founded and was publisher of the Mineral County Miner and South Fork Tines weekly newspaper in Creede and South Fork, Colorado, 1975 - 1981

She is listed in Colorado Newspapers 1935 - 1977.

78235527R00140

Made in the USA
Lexington, KY
06 January 2018